Here's what critics are saying about Gemma Halliday's High Heels Mysteries:

"A saucy combination of romance and suspense that is simply irresistible."
—*Chicago Tribune*

"Stylish…nonstop action…guaranteed to keep chick lit and mystery fans happy!"
—*Publishers' Weekly*, starred review

"Smart, funny and snappy…the perfect beach read!"
—*Fresh Fiction*

"The High Heels Series is amongst one of the best mystery series currently in publication. If you have not read these books, then you are really missing out on a fantastic experience, chock full of nail-biting adventure, plenty of hi-jinks, and hot, sizzling romance. Can it get any better than that?"
—*Romance Reviews Today*

"(A) breezy, fast-paced style, interesting characters and story meant for the keeper shelf. 4 ½!"
—*RT Book Reviews*

"Maddie Springer is like a cross between Paris Hilton and Stephanie Plum, only better. This is one HIGH HEEL you'll want to try on again and again."
—*Romance Junkies*

BOOKS BY GEMMA HALLIDAY

High Heels Mysteries
Spying in High Heels
Killer in High Heels
Undercover in High Heels
Christmas in High Heels
(short story)
Alibi in High Heels
Mayhem in High Heels
Honeymoon in High Heels
(short story)
Sweetheart in High Heels
(short story)
Fearless in High Heels
Danger in High Heels
Homicide in High Heels
Deadly in High Heels
Suspect in High Heels
Peril in High Heels
Jeopardy in High Heels

Wine & Dine Mysteries
A Sip Before Dying
Chocolate Covered Death
Victim in the Vineyard
Marriage, Merlot & Murder
Death in Wine Country
Fashion, Rosé & Foul Play
Witness at the Winery

**Hollywood Headlines
Mysteries**
Hollywood Scandals
Hollywood Secrets
Hollywood Confessions
Hollywood Holiday
(short story)
Hollywood Deception

Marty Hudson Mysteries
Sherlock Holmes and the Case
of the Brash Blonde
Sherlock Holmes and the Case
of the Disappearing Diva
Sherlock Holmes and the Case
of the Wealthy Widow

Tahoe Tessie Mysteries
Luck Be A Lady
Hey Big Spender
Baby It's Cold Outside
(holiday short story)

Jamie Bond Mysteries
Unbreakable Bond
Secret Bond
Bond Bombshell
(short story)
Lethal Bond
Dangerous Bond
Bond Ambition
(short story)
Fatal Bond
Deadly Bond

**Hartley Grace Featherstone
Mysteries**
Deadly Cool
Social Suicide
Wicked Games

Other Works
Play Dead
Viva Las Vegas
A High Heels Haunting
Watching You (short story)
Confessions of a Bombshell
Bandit (short story)

SUSPECT
IN
HIGH HEELS

a High Heels Mystery

GEMMA HALLIDAY

Dedicated to my mom, who would never be caught dead in culottes and is the most fashionable woman I know.

CHAPTER ONE

"If I can get 1,000 bucks for this fertility goddess, I'm taking one heck of a Vegas vacation, baby."

I turned to look at the six-inch green statue in Mrs. Rosenblatt's pudgy hands. It had a bulbous nose, a protruding belly, and a goofy grin on its face that made it look like it'd just downed a double shot of tequila on an empty stomach. If Elmer Fudd was your idea of sexy, this statue had it goin' on.

"If you get a thousand bucks for that, I'm a monkey's aunt," my mom answered, laughing heartily as she voiced my sentiments exactly.

We'd been standing in line for the *Antiques Extravaganza* for the last two hours, and my mom and her best friend were getting a little slaphappy. Me? I was regretting my decision to wear my new Michael Kors pumps. Even though the slim three-inch silver heels were absolutely gorgeous, I would've killed for a chair right about then.

"You just wait, Betty," Mrs. Rosenblatt said, wagging a fingertip—painted bright fuchsia and studded with rhinestones— at my mom. "I know this thing is authentic and worth cash. My fourth husband, Lenny, brought this back with him from a tour of Africa in 1965."

Mrs. Rosenblatt had been married a total of six times, burying three husbands at Forest Lawn Memorial and burying the other three in divorce court. She currently worked as a part-time psychic on the Venice boardwalk—telling fortunes, reading palms, and cleaning dirty auras, and had a collection of muumuus in every color of the rainbow. Eccentric was her middle name.

"I don't know if things from the '60s are actually considered antiques," my mom said. Probably because she predated the era herself.

But Mrs. Rosenblatt waved her off, her underarms continuing to jiggle long after the rest of her had stopped moving. "Nonsense. This thing here is the real deal. I tell you, the week after Lenny brought it home, my niece came over for brisket, saw this sucker, and—*bam!*—she was pregnant with triplets."

I took a small step away from the green statue. Not that I didn't love children. But with my own set of twins, I think I was pretty set in the fertility department.

"What do you think, Maddie?" Mom said, turning to me. "Do you think it's old enough to be considered an antique?"

What I was thinking at the moment was that it was a mistake to have tagged along with these two.

When Mom had first giddily told me that she had secured tickets to the *Antiques Extravaganza* and insisted that I come along with her, I'd been a bit wary but open-minded. Sure, antiquing felt more like something for the AARP set with time on their hands than a busy mom of two running her own shoe design business, but I *had* seen the show on TV, and it *was* kinda fun to guess the values of the kitschy goods people brought in from Grandma's attic. And I *did* have a pair of vintage Chanel two-toned pumps. I wasn't sure that they were worth much as far as the dollar amount went, but it would be interesting to see if the appraisers could give me an idea of their history.

As our tickets had told us, we'd been limited to bringing along just one antique, and Mrs. Rosenblatt had, obviously, chosen her fertility goddess. I had my pumps, and Mom had gone with an antique hatpin decorated in a diamond and ruby floral design that she said had been handed down through the generations of women in her family for the last hundred and fifty years. She'd been keeping it in a safety deposit box since I was twelve and swore that it was "priceless." I warned her that bringing it to the antique show was going to put a price on it.

I shifted from foot to foot as our line moved up by one person. I had a bad feeling the price I was going to be paying for wearing my Michael Kors was blisters the size of silver dollars by the end of the day.

"Look over there!" Mrs. Rosenblatt said.

I glanced in the direction that her fuchsia fingers indicated.

To our right a young woman in a sleek black jumpsuit with gold hoop earrings and a stylish updo sat with the host of the *Antiques Extravaganza*, chatting animatedly over a blue vase with intricately painted cherry blossoms on the side.

"That looks like a celebrity. Where do I know her from?" Mom asked, squinting beneath her powder blue eye shadow—which perfectly matched her baby blue mock turtleneck and pale denim skort. Yes, skort. While I loved my mother with all my heart, no amount of prodding on my part had been able to bring her fashion sense out of the 1980s. I guess I had to give her some credit—it was hard to find a skort for sale these days, so she got points for creative shopping.

"That is a celebrity," Mrs. R said, nodding. "Is it Charlize Theron?"

"I think it is," I responded, honestly as surprised as they were. This didn't really seem like a Hollywood A-lister event.

Beside her, several camera flashes went off as antiquers in the Asian Arts line took photos with their phones. I even spied a blonde woman in a T-shirt that read *L.A. Informer* across the back, indicating she was from one of the local tabloids, popping off a couple of shots.

"Didn't I tell you that antique was the new chic?" Mrs. R said, puffing her chest out triumphantly.

I took a quick glance around at the other antiquing patrons. Sensible shoes, cozy cardigans, and pleated-front slacks seemed to be the predominant look of choice. I wasn't sure if *chic* would be the word I'd use to describe the antiquers, but I had to admit that the celeb sighting did add a bit of cool factor to the outing.

We moved up a step closer, and I peered around my two companions to see just how many more patrons were ahead of us. We were standing in the Jewelry & Accessories line, which seemed to be one of the more popular ones today. I looked longingly over at the Sports Memorabilia line, noting that only three people stood there, and wished I'd brought my husband's baseball card collection instead of my vintage heels.

"If this line moves any slower, we'll be traveling backwards," Mom huffed, shifting her massive purse to the other shoulder. Like a Boy Scout, she believed in being prepared. I was pretty sure her bag held a first aid kit, emergency change of clothes, and possibly even an actual Boy Scout.

"Peter's line always moves slowly," the woman behind us said.

I turned to find a slim lady holding a shopping bag. Her dark brown hair was cut in a severe bob, and her eyes peered at me from behind a pair of large glasses that magnified them to twice their size. She was petite and kind of cute in a quirky way.

"Peter?" Mom asked.

The woman nodded, her glasses slipping down her nose just a bit. "Peter Carrington. The appraiser from Carrington and Cash." She nodded toward the front of the line where a man with dyed black hair in a tweed jacket was pointing out the finer characteristics of a silver brooch to the lucky antiquer at the front of the line. "He's the absolute best. So thorough."

"You've been to the *Antiques Extravaganza* before?" my mom asked.

She nodded again. "I always try to get tickets when they're in town. Of course, Peter's local, so it's a treat when he's here."

"What did you bring to get appraised?" Mrs. Rosenblatt asked, peering into the shopping bag.

The woman's eyes lit up behind her magnified lenses, and she reached her hand into the bag. "Clowns," she said gleefully.

I felt myself jump as her hand emerged with a porcelain clown in a harlequin outfit. The face was contorted into a creepy smile that looked like a cross between the Joker and Chucky.

"That's…unique," Mom said, clearing her throat.

"Thanks." The woman lovingly cradled the creepy doll in her arms. "He's a Burdorf. From Germany."

"Shouldn't you be over in the Toys and Dolls line?" Mrs. Rosenblatt asked.

"Oh no!" Clown Lady shook her head vehemently, her bob whipping back and forth. "This is not a toy. You see the buttons?" She pointed to the items in question down the front of the doll's outfit. "Silver and sapphires. Mr. Bubbles and I can't wait for Peter to see them." She did a big toothy grin that perfectly matched the creepy one on her non-doll.

I mentally shivered. Clowns and I had a history, and it wasn't a pretty one.

Mrs. Rosenblatt squinted down at the little guy. "He looks a lot like my third husband, Alf." She shook her head. "Only Alf was chubbier. He had a glandular problem."

"Would you like to see another one?" Clown Lady asked, her eyes shining. "I brought a few more friends."

Oh boy. This was going to be a *really* long line.

An hour and several more antique brooches, pendants, and handbags later, we finally found ourselves one away from the appraiser. I bounced on my toes as I waited for the woman in front of us to get the rundown on the nineteenth-century gold chain she'd inherited from her great-aunt.

"Well, look at you, Maddie. You look like you're getting excited," Mom said with a knowing glance in my direction.

Actually, I kinda had to pee, but I smiled and nodded at my mother anyway. Who was I to spoil her fun?

A woman wearing a headset and carrying a clipboard interrupted us. "Mr. Carrington will see you now," she told Mom, ushering the three of us forward.

Unlike what I'd seen on television, the majority of the appraisals happening at the *Antiques Extravaganza* were not camera worthy. Peter Carrington sat on a folding chair behind a small table covered in a tablecloth in the show's signature bright blue color. No cameras were currently in residence near him. However, the woman with the headset and clipboard was hovering nearby. While we'd been standing in line, I'd watched Carrington signal to her a couple of times when he apparently thought an antique was a particularly interesting item. The item's owner had then quickly been ushered into a back room, presumably where they were made more "camera ready" and waited for a filmed segment away from the crowded convention center floor.

I could feel Mom practically vibrating with anticipation, hoping she might be one of the lucky few with the ticket into the back rooms.

"It's so nice to meet you, Mr. Carrington," Mom gushed, sticking her hand out toward the man in tweed seated behind the table.

"Charmed." He gave Mom a wan smile and a limp squeeze of her fingers in return. Honestly, he looked bored to tears. However, I could only imagine how many yard sale treasures he'd already appraised. "What have you brought for me today?"

Mom dug her hand into her gargantu-purse and pulled out her lovingly wrapped hatpin. She'd tucked it in tissue, wrapped it in bubble wrap, and stuck it inside a Tyvek envelope. As she peeled back the layers on her gem, she regaled Carrington with the history of the item.

"This was my great-grandmother's grandmother's grandmother's special silver hatpin."

Carrington's ruddy complexion wrinkled as he tried to do the mental math on exactly what generation the piece had come from. Finally, he must've given up, because he said, "That would put it around the time of…"

"1892."

I stifled a laugh. Mom apparently wasn't so big on math herself.

"Uh—" Carrington held up a hand to interrupt.

But Mom was on a roll. "It's been handed down from generation to generation of women in the family ever since then. The legend is that her husband gave it to her on their wedding day as a gift. It had been given to *him* as a gift for his service in the military in the Crimean War. The rubies and diamonds that you see in the floral design actually once belonged to Josephine Bonaparte."

I could see Carrington's bushy eyebrows moving farther and farther toward his receding hairline as Mom's story continued.

"That would be Napoleon's bride," Mrs. Rosenblatt jumped in to clarify.

Carrington shot her a look. "I'm aware of who Josephine Bonaparte is."

"It's a very special piece," my mom finished, finally peeling back the last layer of tissue paper and setting the hatpin down on the table in front of the appraiser.

I had to admit, it was gorgeous. The silver showed some minor signs of aging, but it still gleamed under the bright convention center lights. The rubies and diamonds sparkled in the floral design at the head of the pin, and the long stick extended at least 8 inches, ending in a sharp point that looked deadly enough that I wanted it nowhere near my head.

Carrington picked it up, squinting down at the gems. He turned it over, carefully examining the back and tracing his finger over the worn signature mark of the silversmith who'd created it. Mom held her breath, leaning in closely. I could see her hopefully eyeing the production assistant out of the corner of her eye.

But Carrington didn't call her over. Instead, he set the pin down with a plop on the table in front of him. "It's a reproduction."

Mom sucked in a breath of air on a gasp, her hands going to her chest. "What?"

"What you have here is a cheap modern reproduction of a Regency era pin. These were mass-produced in the 1920s," he said with a dismissive wave of his hand.

"Impossible!" Mom said, her voice going high. "This priceless hatpin has been in my family for several generations. There is no way it was made in the 1920s. Why, my great-great-grandmother wore this on her wedding day in 1901!" Mom shook her head at the man, her cheeks going bright red.

Carrington tilted his head down and looked up at Mom through his sparse eyelashes. "Do you have photographic evidence of this?"

"I…I…"

Carrington smirked. "I didn't think so."

He pushed the hatpin across the table toward Mom, who picked it up and squinted at it, as if trying to see what Carrington was seeing.

"I'm sorry, but this *priceless* family heirloom," he said, the word coming out on a sneer, "is worthless."

Mom sucked in another gasp.

"Even the gems are fake," he added as a final insult.

"Listen, you," Mom said, placing both hands on the table and leaning her face just inches from Carrington's. "Are you calling my great-great-grandmother's grandmother's grandmother a liar?"

Carrington blinked, some of the smug being replaced by fear as he took in the set line of Mom's jaw and her angry slits of eyes. I could see him glancing around to find his production assistant now. "What I'm saying, *ma'am*, is that what you have brought me is costume jewelry easily picked up at a garage sale for under $10."

"Why, you little—"

Mom didn't finish that thought. Instead, I watched in horror as she slid her purse off her shoulder, lifted it high above her head, and swung toward Carrington.

"No!" I shouted, diving for Mom.

"Look out!" the clown lady behind us screamed at Carrington.

"Eep!" Carrington squeaked out, ducking as Mom's bag of tricks sailed just inches over his head.

I grabbed Mom's right arm, and Mrs. Rosenblatt grabbed the left, the two of us just barely able to restrain her from going for another swing as she began throwing curses in Carrington's direction.

"You fraud! You phony! You wouldn't know an antique hatpin if it stuck you in the backside!" she yelled.

I could see production assistants turning toward the commotion, starting to run our direction. In fact, everyone within earshot had turned to see what the screaming was about, including Charlize Theron and the paparazzi photographing her.

That was our cue to leave.

"Let's get her out of here," I mumbled to Mrs. Rosenblatt.

Between the two of us we managed to drag Mom away from Carrington, but not before she had a chance to insult Carrington, his mother, and a goat. By the time we'd dragged her to the bank of chairs along the far wall, the string of curses was making me blush.

"How dare he!" Mom said, letting out a long breath and shaking her head to reposition her feathered bangs.

"Look, let's just calm down for a few minutes," I said, looking over my shoulder for security. We'd be lucky if we weren't thrown out.

"That guy had some nerve." Mrs. Rosenblatt nodded in agreement." I like to give him a piece of my mind."

"No!" I shouted. "No one is giving anyone a piece of anything."

"Did you hear how he insulted your great-great-grandmother's grandmother's grandmother's word?" Mom said, turning to me. The anger had receded from her face, and I now saw tears backing up behind her eyes.

I shook my head. "Clearly he was mistaken," I told her. Though whether I believed that or not, I wasn't sure. The truth was, my great-great-grandmother hadn't been all together there at the end. Honestly? There was a good chance Carrington was right about the hatpin. "Maybe we should just go."

"What about my fertility goddess?" Mrs. Rosenblatt said, holding up the Green Goblin. "I haven't got it appraised yet."

I took a deep breath. I counted to 10. "Fine. We'll get the fertility thing appraised."

"Goddess"

"Whatever." I did another 5 count, but it wasn't doing much good. "Look, maybe we should just take a few minutes to get something to eat and cool off." And I still really had to go to the bathroom.

Mom nodded. "It is lunchtime."

Having diffused that bomb, I sent Mom and Mrs. Rosenblatt toward the concession stands set up in a smaller room off the main convention hall as I went to find the nearest restroom.

I took care of business, freshened up my Raspberry Perfection lip gloss, and did a couple of powder puffs at the sheen that had developed on my forehead during Mom's altercation. Then I left the ladies' room and found a quiet hallway to quickly check in on the twins, who were at home under the watchful eye of my best friend, Dana.

Dana Dashel and I had been joined at the hip since junior high, having gone through the awkwardness of high school together as well as the struggles of adulting—me starting a career as a footwear fashion designer and her spending years as a struggling actress-slash-almost-everything-else. Luckily, those days were mostly behind us, as I was finally designing my own collections for fancy boutiques in Beverly Hills, and Dana was landing actual paying roles on TV and film on a regular basis.

I swiped my cell on and waited while the phone rang on the other end. And rang. And rang. Just when I was sure it was about to go to voicemail, I heard my bestie's voice pick up.

"Maddie?" Dana said, clearly out of breath.

"Yeah, it's me," I told her. "Where was it this time?"

I heard Dana chuckle on the other end. "Top rack of the dishwasher."

I laughed out loud. Recently, Max, the male half of my two-year-old twins, had taken to hiding cell phones. I had a feeling he was trying to tell us something about our inattentiveness as parents. But now it had become a game, and we were never quite sure where the ringing would come from in the house. "Good thing you didn't run a load."

"With these two around? I'm lucky to be able to find the dishwasher, let alone use it."

I grinned again. Parenthood was a never dull journey. "So how are the monsters doing?" I asked.

"Oh, they're fine. Ricky, however, might need a stiff drink when we're done."

Ricky Montgomery was Dana's boyfriend as well as a rising Hollywood star. He and Dana had met when we'd been undercover on the set of his TV show, and he'd publicly proposed to Dana on the air in one of the most romantic moments I'd ever been fortunate enough to witness. However, that had been over two years ago. And he was still dragging his feet about setting a wedding date. In an effort to push him toward domestic life, Dana had volunteered the two of them to babysit the twins while I'd gone antiquing.

"Is Ricky okay?" I asked, putting my finger to my other ear to block out the dull hum of noise from the convention center floor.

"Oh yeah," Dana assured me. "He's fine. Tired. And he's learned the hard way not to ever wear Armani around a potty-training toddler." She stifled a giggle on the other end. "But everything's cool here. How's the *Extravaganza*?"

I gave her the CliffsNotes version of our adventure so far. By the time I got to Mom threatening Carrington, she was in all-out laughter.

"Sounds like your two are even more trouble than these two," she said. "By the way…"

I strained to hear her as her voice trailed off.

"Sorry. I'm having a hard time hearing you," I said, realizing how true that was. Somehow the dull hum of noise around me had risen to mild roar status.

"I just wondered how…Max should get…or is there something else?"

"What?" I yelled into my phone. I stepped out of the hallway onto the main floor, and the hairs on the back of my neck started to stand on end. The noise had reached a deafening level, converging around one of the back rooms I'd seen lucky patrons with unique items being pulled into. Someone was shouting for security, people with clipboards were running back and forth like headless chickens, and I noticed several women sobbing.

"Um, I'm having a hard time hearing you. I'll call you back," I told Dana, swiping my phone off.

I grabbed the arm of a woman in a headset as she bustled past me.

"Excuse me, what's going on?"

Her face was pale. "It's Carrington." She gulped audibly, eyes darting side to side, almost as if she wasn't sure she should say the words out loud.

But finally she did.

"He's dead."

CHAPTER TWO

————

If there was anything in this world worse than standing in a two-hour line next to a woman holding a bag full of clowns, it was standing in a room full of antsy antiquers waiting to be questioned by the police as possible eyewitnesses in a murder.

The giddy excitement in the air had turned to solemn whisperers and suspicious glances as the police now used the existing lines to question possible witnesses instead of appraising antiques.

"Excuse me, ma'am?"

I looked up to find a tall police officer in a blue uniform addressing my mom. He had a shock of red hair, and his face was covered in a fine dusting of pale freckles.

"Y-yes?" she asked on a shaky voice.

"The detective would like to speak with you. Could you please come to the front of the line?"

"Well, it's about time!" Mrs. Rosenblatt cut in. "My corns are killing me."

Officer Freckles' eyebrows pinched together momentarily, as if trying to erase that mental picture. However, he gently led Mom forward by the elbow to the front of the line.

"Isn't it nice that we're getting some preferential treatment?" Mom whispered to me, giving me a wink.

I wasn't so sure. In my experience, there was only one reason a homicide detective wanted to talk to you…and it wasn't a good one.

I realized soon enough why we had been called to the front of the line, as the officer led us to a booth that had been sectioned off by blue curtains with a sign above reading *Porcelain Appraisals*. As the officer pulled aside the curtains, I saw it had been turned into a makeshift interrogation room. A plainclothes detective sat on one side of a folding table, which was still covered in small porcelain miniature figures, most of them in various states of undress. A boy looked like he was peeing into a fake fountain, a Venus Di Milo look-alike bore her breasts on a half shell, and two figurines in jade were wrapped up in each other in what I could only interpret as the aftereffects of a fertility goddess statue. The whole thing might have even been slightly comical if I hadn't known the detective sitting behind the table. Intimately.

Detective Jack Ramirez was tall, dark, and dangerously handsome. He also happened to be my husband.

"Hi, honey," I squeaked out, doing a little one finger wave in his direction.

All I got back was a grunt. Clearly he was not happy to be here.

His dark hair curled just a couple weeks past needing a haircut at the nape of his neck, and his normally brown eyes were almost black as they homed in on me from his unreadable Cop Face. His jaw was clenched, and a little vein was threatening to bulge at the side of his neck as he stared me down.

Officer Freckles indicated a trio of folding chairs for the three of us to sit on, and then he hightailed it out of there. Lucky Officer Freckles. I itched to join him.

"Oh, Jack, thank goodness you're here," Mom gushed at him, clearly not used to being on the business end of Cop Face. "They're saying that appraiser is dead!"

Ramirez cleared his throat, his expression softening a little as he turned it on my mom. "Unfortunately, they are right."

Mom and Mrs. Rosenblatt gasped as one.

Ramirez looked at me, his expression a perfectly intimidating poker face. "You wouldn't happen to know anything about this, would you?"

"Who, me?" I asked in my most innocent voice. Which wasn't too difficult to pull off, since I actually *was* innocent. Clearly, I hadn't had anything to do with the death of the grouchy appraiser. But the truth was, this was not the first time I had ever found a dead body. In fact, my friends had started to joke that I was a bit of a dead body magnet. It totally wasn't my fault. You know how some people have all the luck when it comes to snagging great parking at the mall or hitting the ATM at just the right time to avoid any lines? I mean, you don't blame them for always getting the prime parking places or fast cash, right? So it was totally not my fault that I just happened to be in the vicinity of people when they happened to be murdered by other people. I mean, it wasn't like I actually caused any of these murders myself. I was an innocent bystander.

That was my story, and I was sticking to it.

Unfortunately it was a story my husband had heard several times. And he'd never been a fan of it.

"I'm guessing the fact that you're here means that he didn't kill himself, right?" I asked my husband.

He nodded, his jaw tight. "It's being investigated as a death under suspicious circumstances," he said, giving us the standard line.

I steeled myself for more questioning, but instead he turned toward Mom. "You knew the appraiser?"

"M-me?" she stammered, clearly not ready for the question.

"I'm told you had a conversation with him prior to his death?"

"Conversation" was a nice way of putting it. I felt a slight unpleasant niggling in my gut that my husband wasn't asking for no reason. Mom had had a rather loud argument with the man. Right before he'd been killed. But surely no one would think Mom had anything to do with—

"Wait—you don't think I had anything to do with this?" Mom asked. For all her quirks, Mom was one smart cookie.

"Me?" Ramirez asked, putting a hand to his chest. "No. I know you didn't have anything to do with this, Betty."

I narrowed my eyes at my husband. "But…"

Ramirez sighed, as if he was wishing he was anywhere but there. "But, several witnesses came forward saying that you had an altercation with Mr. Carrington just before the victim expired."

"It was just a silly argument," I jumped in. I paused, something occurring to me. "Security cameras!"

Ramirez turned to me.

"Surely you can check the security cameras. They were all over the place." I'd noticed several near the various booths as I'd stood in line.

But Ramirez shook his head. "There were cameras, but they were specifically trained on the booths and tables. Carrington was killed in one of the back rooms."

Drat. So much for that.

Ramirez turned to my mom. "So, I have to ask, what was that argument about?"

Mom bit her lip. It was a habit I was ashamed to say I'd inherited from her. I resisted the urge to nibble my lip gloss right off along with her.

"It was about her hatpin," Mrs. Rosenblatt supplied. "That smarmy snake of a phony appraiser said it was fake."

Ramirez raised an eyebrow in her direction. "A hatpin?"

Something in the way he said it made that niggle in my belly turn into a full-blown rumbling. "Why do you ask?"

But he ignored me, turning again to Mom. "I take it you disagreed with Carrington's appraisal?"

"Darn tooting!" Mrs. Rosenblatt said, nodding supportively toward Mom, who still wasn't saying much. "That hatpin has been in her family for generations. It's an heirloom. That man wouldn't know real diamonds if they came out of his rear—"

"Please," Mom cut her off just in time. "The man is dead."

Ramirez coughed. If I had to guess, it was to cover a laugh.

"But it's true about the appraisal," Mom said, nodding, her feathered bangs bobbing up and down on her head. "He was completely mistaken."

"And, he was completely alive when we left him," I added for emphasis.

Ramirez cleared his throat. "Okay, take me through what you did next."

"Well, I—" I started.

But Ramirez cut me off. "Not you, Maddie."

I shut my mouth with a click, turning to Mom.

Her eyes darted between us, clearly not comfortable with all of the scrutiny. "Well...Dorothy and I," she said, nodding in Mrs. Rosenblatt's direction, "went to go get something to eat. Soft pretzels. You know, to calm down and regroup before we got into the Sculptures line to get her fertility goddess appraised."

Ramirez's eyes went up again.

"She's African," Mrs. Rosenblatt filled him in. "One look at her is all it takes to get a girl knocked up."

Ramirez did a cover-up cough again. "Okay, so you went to go get pretzels. Together, correct?"

Mom and Mrs. Rosenblatt both nodded vigorously.

"There was no point where you left each other's sides, correct?"

Mom and Mrs. Rosenblatt both stop nodding. They shared a sidelong glance at each other.

Uh-oh.

"Well..." Mom started.

"Well what? Do you have an alibi or not?" I asked, getting antsy.

Ramirez shot me a look that clearly said *Ixnay on the interrogation-nay*. I made a zipping-my-mouth-shut-and-throwing-away-the-key motion.

"Well," Mom said again. "The pretzels made Dorothy thirsty. So she did get up to go get a frozen lemonade at one point. But she came right back. It was only a couple of minutes."

Ramirez let out a deep sigh, leaning back in his chair.

While this hole in Mom's alibi wasn't good, I could tell by the look on Ramirez's face that there was something else too.

"What?" I asked him.

He looked up and locked eyes with mine for just a moment. This time it wasn't his Cop Face. It was the face of a husband who felt terrible about the news he was about to break to his wife.

Double uh-oh.

Ramirez turned to Mom. "Tell me more about the hatpin that you had appraised by the victim."

"Uh, well, it was silver."

Ramirez closed his eyes, his eyebrows drawing together in a frown. "It didn't happen to have a flower shape at one end with some gems in it, did it?"

"Why do you ask?" I jumped in.

Ramirez opened his eyes and gave me that sympathetic look again. "Because that's exactly what the murder weapon looked like."

Mom and Mrs. Rosenblatt did the simultaneous gasp thing again. In fact, I might have joined them, the air suddenly collapsing out of my chest.

I felt my eyes ping-pong between Ramirez and Mom. "It couldn't have been. Mom, you put the hatpin back into your purse, right?"

"I-I thought I did." She bit her lip again, turning to Mrs. Rosenblatt. "Dorothy, I did put it into my purse, right?"

Mrs. Rosenblatt's massive shoulders jumped up and down, making the hibiscus on her muumuu dance. "Sure. I mean, where else would you put it?"

"Did you have your purse with you the whole time? Did you set it down anywhere? Are you sure you put the hatpin in? Could you have left it at the appraisal table? Could it have fallen out?" I felt myself starting to hyperventilate.

"Calm down. Breathe," Ramirez instructed.

I shut my mouth and breathed deeply through my nose. I heard Mom and Mrs. Rosenblatt doing the same thing beside me.

When I finally got my breath under control, I turned to my husband. "Jack, you don't seriously believe that my mom had anything to do with this?"

There was that sympathetic look again. I was starting to miss Cop Face. "Your mother was in an altercation with the victim moments before he was killed. With a murder weapon that belongs to her. At this point, Maddie, I'm not sure it matters what I believe."

* * *

After assuring me that he'd do everything he could to look into what really happened, Ramirez cleared us to go home as he stayed behind to sort out the mess. While part of me itched to know what the crime scene techs swabbing every surface of the appraisal tables where uncovering, I knew that the most helpful thing I could do was get Mom home and let my husband do his job.

I spent the better part of the car ride grilling my mom about just how the hatpin had escaped her purse. The truth was, none of us had been paying that close attention to our belongings at the time, all three of us riled up by the argument with Carrington. But Mom swore she hadn't seen anyone near her purse. Apparently she did realize how incriminating that statement looked for her.

I dropped Mom off at home and Mrs. Rosenblatt off at the senior center in Santa Monica, and was treated to the comforting sounds of utter chaos as I walked to the front door of my own bungalow in West LA. I could hear Max screaming something about flinging boogers, and Livvie, the female half of my twins, screaming something about *catching* boogers, and Ricky screaming that if anyone flung anything again, they were sitting in time-out.

"Honeys, I'm home," I called, carefully setting my vintage shoes down on the entryway table as I walked into the eye of the storm.

Immediately screams ceased from two out of three directions, and Livvie and Max attacked my legs with hugs, kisses, and little pudgy fingers. I had to admit that after the afternoon I'd had, it was more than welcome. I knelt down and returned the hugs and kisses and added in just a couple belly farts for good measure. Once the twins had had their fill, they ran off happily toward the sound of Mickey Mouse from the TV in the back bedroom.

I straightened up to find my babysitters looking a bit worse for the wear. Ricky's normally artfully tousled hair was *actually* tousled, standing on end and possibly caked with a little yogurt on one side. There was a suspicious stain on his pants, and it looked like Livvie had applied red marker to his fingernails. And his fingers. (We were working on hand-eye coordination.) Dana didn't look too much better—barefoot, strawberry blonde hair in a messy bun, a brown streak of ambiguous origin across one cheek, standing in the middle of a tiny-person tornado that included toys, Cheerios, juice cups, and discarded clothing. If I had to guess, an afternoon with my kids hadn't so much pushed Ricky toward domestic bliss as it had given Dana second thoughts.

"How were they?" I asked. Though the scene in front of me pretty much answered that question.

"Who? The little—" Ricky started.

"Angels," Dana finished, sending him a pointed look. "They were little angels."

I grinned. For an actress, my best friend was a terrible liar. "Glad to hear it."

"You're home early," Dana said, glancing at the clock.

"Not early enough." I sighed.

As we cleaned up the chaos in the living room, I filled Dana and Ricky in on what had happened at the *Antiques Extravaganza*. Not that I had a lot of details, other than my mom had *not* killed the appraiser and all signs pointed to the idea that she had.

Dana and Ricky made the appropriate gasps and wide eyes at all the right parts.

"So, you think someone stole your mom's hatpin and killed the guy with it?" Dana asked when I'd finished.

I shrugged. "They must have."

"Do you think it was opportunity or intentional?" Ricky asked, collapsing onto the sofa.

"You mean, do I think someone actually framed my mom on purpose?" That was a disconcerting thought.

Ricky nodded. "Or maybe the hatpin just looked convenient?"

I shook my head. "I don't know. But the argument she had with the victim was loud enough that almost anyone there would have heard it. She makes a good scapegoat."

"The police can't possibly think your mother had anything to do with this!" Dana jumped in, her brows pulling down in a frown of concern.

I shrugged. "It doesn't look good."

"But *Ramirez* knows she had nothing to do with it, right?" she pressed.

I nodded. "Absolutely. And I'm sure he'll do what he can, but I just don't know how much that will be."

My concern lacing that thought must have been clear on my face, as Dana patted my hand reassuringly. "I'm sure your mom will be fine. I mean, if this guy Carrington was that much of a jerk, chances are he's cheesed off a whole list of antiquers, right?"

"Right," I said, liking that idea. "I'm sure Mom's not the first person he's rubbed the wrong way."

Ricky pulled his phone out of his pocket. "Let's check it out," he said pulling up social media sites.

Dana and I watched over his shoulder as he scrolled through several different articles about Carrington, most of them about his untimely demise that afternoon.

"Looks like he was local," Ricky said, pulling up a social media page with Carrington's picture front and center. "It says here he co-owned a small antique shop in Venice called Yesterday's Treasures."

"We should totes go there tomorrow," Dana said, bobbing her bun up and down.

I gave her a look. Something about the hint of excitement in her voice made me think she's wasn't just interested in the antiques.

"What?" she said with mock innocence. "You want your mom to go down for murder?"

"Dana!" Ricky nudged her with his elbow. "I'm sure Ramirez won't let that happen."

But I knew a small part of her was right. Of course my husband would do everything he could to keep Mom out of trouble. But with a roomful of witnesses to their altercation and the murder weapon in her possession, I wasn't sure if everything he could do would be enough.

"I guess it wouldn't hurt to just go ask a couple of questions…" I trailed off.

"I'll be here at nine," Dana said.

CHAPTER THREE

———————

The next morning Ramirez was up and out the door before I even had the willpower to raise my head off the pillow. Not that he expected it of me. He'd known when we'd met that I was not an early riser, and he accepted it just like I accepted the fact he'd never learn to put the toilet seat down. Call it marital compromise. Especially since the twins had come along, I'd taken advantage of every second of sleep I could get. Even if those seconds were usually over much too quickly. Case in point—almost as soon as I heard Ramirez's car start up in the driveway, giggles sounded over the baby monitor.

As much as I wanted to pull the covers over my head, I knew that ten more minutes of beauty sleep was out of the question. Luckily, along with giggling, I could detect the faint scents of coffee from the kitchen. Ramirez had made a pot before leaving. Bless that man. You see why I could let the toilet seat thing slide.

I rubbed my eyes with my fist and yawned as I shuffled down the hallway and into the twins' room. When I stepped through the door, I flicked on the overhead light and saw Livvie wide-eyed and laughing over the rail of her crib. Max had his face pressed between the wooden slats of his bed, the most mischievous grin I had ever seen plastered on his chubby little face. If he hadn't been in his crib all night, I'd be more than a little suspicious as to what he'd been up to. No one in the world could be that cute and that happy with themselves and *not* have been up to something.

I quickly diapered and dressed them—Livvie in a sweet pink floral outfit with big heart-shaped buttons lining the front, and Max in a pair of blue shorts and matching baby blue button-down shirt. I capped their outfits off with shoes from Tot Trots, the company where'd I'd started my shoe design career putting out character themed footwear for kids. Luckily, my clientele had advanced from toddlers to Hollywood housewives, but I still enjoyed a good pair of Spiderman sandals now and then. For Max, of course.

I plopped the cutesome twosome down in the living room with some Cheerios, juice, and Elmo on the TV, and headed toward the luscious aroma of French Roast.

Half an hour later, I'd managed a shower, a loose ponytail, and some foundation, mascara, and lip gloss. I threw on an extra layer of concealer to cover the early morning lurking beneath my eyes and grabbed a navy blue wrap skirt and a white cap sleeve top. I was just adding a pair of neutral wedge sandals when the doorbell rang. I checked my bedside clock. Nine on the dot.

I opened the door to find Dana on my porch with two cups of Starbucks in her hands.

"You are a goddess," I told her.

"I *am* a goddess—thanks for noticing—and I'm all yours until noon."

"What's at noon?" I asked, ushering her in as the *Sesame Street* theme song signaled the end of the episode and the end of relative quiet from the twins. I grabbed one cup from her and the remote in the other hand, quickly putting on another show before a Cheerio food fight broke out.

"I've got to meet with caterers to decide if we want to go with an Asian street fair theme or an Ethiopian finger food theme for Ricky's party." In her ongoing effort to push Ricky toward wedded bliss, Dana had decided to throw her boyfriend a surprise birthday party. What might have been an intimate get-together to start with had begun to spiral out of control into a full-blown event of the season. She'd even hired our mutual friend, Marco, to be her party-planner extraordinaire. And if there was one thing that Marco was good at, over-the-top spiraling was it.

"If I have a vote," I told her, "I say go spicy."

"Duly noted," Dana said, sipping at her coffee. "So, what's the plan today?" she asked, changing gears. "Case the antique place? Interrogate the employees? Hack the victim's files?"

I shot her a look. "What are you, Magnum PI? We're not casing or hacking anything."

Dana looked mildly disappointed. "Maybe just a little interrogating then?"

I couldn't help but grin. Dana was between acting jobs, and I could tell she was getting into the role of Dana Dashel, Private Investigator. If nothing else, her choice of wardrobe gave it away—a pair of dark boots, black pantsuit, and a trench coat that was completely out of place for a summer day in Los Angeles. We'd be lucky if the heat index didn't hit 90 today.

"First," I told her, shoving a couple of bags of goldfish into a diaper bag, "we're going to drop the twins off at preschool."

She frowned. Clearly that was not in her action-adventure script.

"Then, we're going to take my pair of vintage heels down to Yesterday's Treasures to see if they can tell me what the shoes might be worth."

Dana nodded. "And then we'll interrogate."

"We *might, possibly ask* a couple of questions about Carrington. Discreetly."

"Right. Discreet." She gave me an exaggerated wink.

Oh boy. I had a bad feeling discreet wasn't in her script either.

One more episode of Elmo, a few more Cheerios, and a change of outfit for Max (due to an orange juice related accident) later, I finally had two kids, one blonde bombshell, and a third cup of coffee to-go in my minivan. We arrived at preschool five minutes late, but better late than covered in schmutz, as Mrs. Rosenblatt always said.

Traffic was thankfully lighter than normal on the 405, and twenty minutes later we were parking at the curb beside Yesterday's Treasures. It was housed in a trendy block near the beach, in a modern looking stucco building that felt completely incongruent with the wares inside but totally on point with the juice bars and tanning salons lining the street. A gray sign with raised black lettering touted the business's name above the door, and the window held a display of midcentury furniture mixed with Victorian apparel and Italianate artwork.

As we pushed through the glass doors to the shop, I wasn't sure what I expected, but the sign on the door reading *Open* and the clean, sunny looking interior held no hint of the tragedy that had befallen the co-owner the day before. Bright overhead lighting shone on the jam-packed shop, every inch of which was filled with antique furniture, vintage clothes, and cases of jewelry and collectibles. The walls were lined with framed paintings and woven tapestries, and several glass cases held collections of art, antique weapons, and dainty porcelain figures. Everywhere I turned sat sparkling little gems of history, and it was hard to know where to look first, my eyes darting to take it all in. They finally landed on a case filled with old jewelry, diamonds winking up at me from the funky art deco settings.

"Gorgeous," Dana breathed beside me, seemingly in the same state of overwhelmed awe as she looked down at a delicate tennis bracelet set in white gold.

I nodded in agreement. "With a price to match," I noted, taking in the five-figure tag tucked discreetly beside the item.

"Welcome to Yesterday's Treasures."

I looked up to find a tall, slender young woman with long auburn hair and green catlike eyes approaching us.

"Is there something I can help you with today?" she asked, a pleasant customer service smile pasted on her face.

I glanced down at the tag on her lapel that read *Mina*. "Uh, yes, actually. I have these shoes." I held up the box holding my Chanels.

"Are you looking to sell them?" she asked.

I nodded. "Possibly. I was hoping to get an idea of what they're worth first."

Mina nodded. "Sure. Let's see what we can do." She waved us to follow her toward a counter near the back. Her long bohemian skirt swished around her calves as she walked, and her flats whispered gently across the polished hardwood floor. Once she rounded the counter, I sat the box down on top of the long glass case and removed the lid.

"1960s Chanel," I told her. I adored the shoes, but as much as I felt they were works of art, actually wearing them was something I seldom did. If Mina quoted me a high enough price, I actually might sell them.

She gently removed a shoe from the box. "Two-tone. Originals. Very beautiful," she mused and turned it over in her hands. "These look like they're in fabulous condition."

"Thank you. I took them to the *Antiques Extravaganza* yesterday in hopes of securing an appraisal," I began. "But before I could talk to Mr. Carrington…" I let the sentence trail, hoping Mina would pick up where I left off.

"Yes." She nodded, her eyes going to the floor. "His passing," she said simply.

I supposed *his passing* was easier for some to say than *his murder*.

"I'm sorry for your loss," Dana jumped in. "You must have known him well?"

Mina shrugged as she placed my shoe back in its box, some of the excitement at seeing the heels leaving her posture. "He owns this place. Or did," she corrected herself awkwardly.

"Have you worked here long?"

"A couple semesters. I'm getting my degree in art history, so all of this is right up my alley. I kinda love it." She swept her hand around to encompass the contents of the shop.

"I can see why," I said, honestly, thinking of the case of vintage jewelry.

"Do you know if Carrington had any family?" Dana asked. "Wife or girlfriend?"

Mina shook her head. "No, he was single. No girlfriend that I know of, and he never mentioned any family. Why?"

"How was Carrington to work for?" Dana pressed on. "Hard? Stingy? Difficult?"

Mina frowned again.

I shot Dana a look. PI Girl was pushing it.

"He was…fine," she finally said.

Dana frowned, clearly not getting the dramatic answer she was after. "How did he get along with his customers?" she asked.

"F-fine," Mina repeated. "I mean, since the TV show came along, he's been too busy to be in the shop much. But his celebrity status has really helped bring in more business in the last few months. I usually run the shop stuff, but Mr. Carrington and Ms. Cash are out doing appraisals a lot."

"Ms. Cash?" I asked. I recognized the name as the second half of the victim's Carrington and Cash Appraisals.

"Oh, uh, Allison Cash. She's the other owner. She and Mr. Carrington are business partners. Well, *were* business partners," she corrected herself again.

"How did she get along with Carrington?" Dana asked.

Mina blinked at her. "Uh…fine."

"Is Ms. Cash in?" I asked, peeking around the woman toward a door marked *Offices*.

Mina nodded. "Sure. Um, why? Did you need to speak to her?" She pulled that frown again.

I opened my mouth to respond, but PI Girl ran right over me.

"We'd like to offer our condolences. You see, my friend, here was actually one of the last people to see Mr. Carrington alive." Dana gestured toward me with a dramatic flourish.

"I, uh, well, was one of many at the show…" I hedged.

Mina nodded. "I'll see if Allison is free," she promised, edging away from us.

"Dramatic much?" I asked when Mina was out of earshot.

"Thanks." Dana grinned at me.

I didn't have the heart to tell her it wasn't exactly a compliment.

A moment later, Mina reappeared from the back rooms. "Ms. Cash is just finishing up with a client. She'll be out in just a minute if you'd like to wait."

"Thanks," I told her, tucking my shoebox back under my arm.

As we moved away from the counter, the bell over the front door tinkled, and another customer walked in.

Mina's face brightened immediately. "Mrs. LaMore! Lovely to see you again."

Mrs. LaMore was a short, round woman wearing a green polyester pantsuit that clung in all the wrong places. It might have flirted with trendy in the seventies, but it was far from retro chic. Her hair was a deep orange and was partially covered in a matching green felt hat with a floppy brim, and what she lacked in youth she made up for in makeup, her eyes rimmed in a pair of the thickest eyelashes I'd seen outside of a Maybelline campaign. She held a heavy looking item wrapped in paper in her arms, huffing it toward the counter, where she plopped it down in front of Mina.

"Hello, dahling," she said in a voice laced with at least twenty years of cigarette smoke. "I've got a real gem to show you today." She paused, giving a cursory nod at Dana and me. "That is, if I'm not interrupting."

I shook my head. "Oh, no, we're waiting to see Ms. Cash."

"Ah." She glanced at my shoebox. "You selling those or buying?"

"Selling. Possibly," I added, still not 100% sure I was ready to part with them.

"Mrs. LaMore is a regular here," Mina told me.

"Please, I've told you a thousand times to call me Lottie," she admonished Mina. "And really, it was my husband who was the regular, God rest his soul."

"I'm so sorry," I told her. "He passed recently?"

"Six months ago. Heart attack. But he managed to amass quite the antique collection before he went. Louis loved anything with a history. He saw true beauty where all others see is yard sale fodder."

"Is this one of his collection?" I asked, gesturing to her package.

Lottie nodded, her hat bobbing. "Yes! Quite a gem, really. Ever heard of the Heffernan Studios?"

I shook my head, admitting I had not.

Lottie frowned, looking a bit put out. "Well, it was *the* place to be in the sixties. All the great modern artists of the era came out of there. This is an Alvero Dilama!" she said with flourish, peeling back paper.

I looked at the large, oddly shaped lump of glazed clay. I tilted my head, not sure if it was upside down. I was almost certain I'd seen an exact replica last week when I'd bought Max and Livvie a tub of Play-Doh.

"What is it?" I asked.

"Art!" Lottie replied.

"It's…very unique," Dana said.

"Isn't it?" Lottie said proudly. "So thought provoking. So symbolic. So…"

Preschool-esque?

"…breathtaking!" she finished with a contented sigh.

"And you're selling it today?" I asked.

Lottie shrugged, pushing the blob along the counter toward Mina. "Possibly. I wanted to see what kind of price Allison might give me." She paused. "When I had it appraised yesterday, they told me it would fetch at least fifty thousand retail."

I blinked at the lump of clay, suddenly wondering what I could sell Max's creations for.

"Yesterday?" Dana jumped in. "That wouldn't happen to have been at the *Antiques Extravaganza*, would it?"

"Well, yes. I always try to go when they're in town."

"Did Carrington appraise this?" I asked.

"Oh, no." Lottie shook her head. "He was doing accessories yesterday, I believe. I was in the pottery line. I really didn't even see him. And then…" She trailed off, eyes going to the ground. "Terrible business." She paused, looking up at Mina through her lashes. "But I know he would have liked this sculpture."

"Uh, let's have Ms. Cash look at it, shall we?" Mina answered very noncommittally.

Lottie shrugged. "Yes, I think that's a good idea."

"Why don't you follow me to the register, and we'll do some paperwork."

The older woman nodded, and the two moved toward the back, leaving the so-called masterpiece on the counter. I stared at it again, trying to find the symbolism in it. I guessed beauty really was in the eye of the beholder.

"Mina said you wanted to speak with me?"

I looked up to find a slim, petite woman wearing a pair of black cigarette pants, black pointy-toed boots, and a black shirt buttoned all the way up to her neck, stepping from the back room. She wore her jet black hair in a short pixie haircut, and the look on her face was about as sunny as her outfit—eyes sharp and assessing, mouth drawn into a fine line slashed with red lipstick, jaw set at a hard angle.

"Ms. Allison Cash?" I asked, stepping forward.

She nodded curtly. "Yes."

"I'm Maddie Springer, and this is my friend, Dana Dashel." I offered my hand to her, which she shook with a quick, icy grip.

"Mina said you had something to sell us?" she asked, coming right to the point.

I nodded, handing her my shoebox. "Possibly. I was hoping to get an idea what they're worth first."

Allison opened the box, pulling one shoe out and inspecting it.

"I wanted to have them appraised at the *Antiques Extravaganza* yesterday but didn't get the chance," I explained, hoping to segue to talking about Carrington as easily as I had with her employee.

"Yes," she said without the least bit of emotion. "We're all deeply saddened by that business."

She sounded as if she were talking about a skinny profit margin and not the death of her business partner. But people grieved in all different ways, I reminded myself, trying not to be too quick to judge.

"You don't seem very broken up about it," Dana blurted out. Clearly she had already judged and jury-ed.

Allison Cash blinked at us. "We're all very saddened by it," she repeated. Though it held more of a defensive tone than anything akin to sad.

"I'm sorry for your loss," I said quickly.

"Thank you," Allison said curtly.

"I was actually in his line for an appraisal yesterday," I said again. "I had hoped to speak with him."

Allison waved it off. "These are simple enough to put a price on," she assured me.

I wasn't sure how I felt about my vintage Chanel being called *simple*, but I nodded. "Any idea what they may be worth?"

She shrugged. "They're in fairly good condition. Some minor wear along the soles, and a couple of scuffs here," she said, pointing to the instep.

"Well, they are old," I said, feeling defensive.

"Hmm," she said, still turning the shoes over in her hands.

"How long were you and Carrington partners?" Dana asked.

"I suppose we've been in business together for a little over a year."

"Strictly business?" Dana asked.

Allison's head popped up. "Excuse me?"

I elbowed Dana in the ribs.

"Uh, what I meant was that you two got along?"

"Yes." She narrowed her eyes. "Why wouldn't we?"

"He was murdered," Dana pointed out. "Someone didn't get along with him—*ouch*!"

I might have elbowed a tad harder that time.

"Look, if you're insinuating something about Peter's death—"

"Of course we're not," I quickly covered. "We just wanted to pay our proper condolences."

"You know, to whomever was closest with him," Dana pressed, scooting out of range of my elbows. Smart girl.

"I wouldn't know," Allison answered in a clipped tone. "His personal life was his business."

"Were you at the *Extravaganza* with him?" Dana asked.

Allison shook her head. "Something came up at the last minute yesterday, and I was not able to attend."

I waited for more about what the *something* was, but she just shoved the shoebox toward me across the counter. "I can offer you fifty dollars."

I choked back my shock at the low price. "Fifty dollars? For vintage Chanel?"

Allison shrugged. "They're nowhere near mint condition. The market is soft on clothing right now, and I'd have to make a profit. I have refurbishment and storage costs, not to mention auction fees."

"Auction fees?"

She nodded. "These won't fetch much retail. They need a specific buyer. We usually list with Van Steinberg's, and they'll want their cut for the advertising."

I tucked the tissue around heels and carefully placed the lid. "I'll have to think about it," I told her, swallowing down my disappointment.

Allison shrugged. "Suit yourself. The offer stands. It's more than fair."

I doubted that. In fact, I had a feeling Allison was lowballing me. Whether it was standard business practice for her or whether it was due to my friend's interrogation, I wasn't sure.

* * *

"So, what do we think of the partner's act?" Dana said once we'd left the building.

I shot her a look. "*If* it was an act."

"Sure. If." Dana winked at me.

This time I didn't even try to restrain the eye roll. "What I think is that Allison is a very tolerant person."

"How so?" Dana frowned.

"She didn't call security on you." I grinned at her.

"Ha. Ha. Very funny," Dana said. Though she was smiling at my teasing. "But seriously. She didn't seem very broken up about the death."

"No," I admitted, "she didn't. But why kill him?"

"Maybe the business is in trouble. Maybe Carrington wanted to dissolve the partnership. Maybe she just hated the guy."

"That's a lot of maybes."

Dana frowned. "It is a few, huh?" She picked up her phone, scrolling through some pages. "What we need is someone who really knew what the relationship between the two business partners was like."

"What we *need* is to leave this to Ramirez. We were just asking a few questions, remember?"

Dana shot me a *get real* look. "You're seriously going to do nothing while the police suspect your mom and a real killer roams the streets, possibly ready to strike again?"

PI Girl was going for that dramatic flair again. However, beneath the sensationalism, I had to admit, she had a good point. Any other day, I might have walked away, but it was my *mom* we were talking about…

"You really think Carrington and Cash might have been on the outs with each other?" I asked.

Dana grinned, knowing she had me. "I think people with good working relationships show some remorse when the other dies."

"Mina said they seemed to get along fine," I said.

"Yeah, according to Mina, everything is 'fine.' What else is she going to say if she likes her job?"

"True. So who else would know if there was any bad blood between the two?"

"I say we start with Van Steinberg," Dana said, eyes on her phone.

"Who?"

She flipped her phone around so I could see the screen. "Van Steinberg's Auction House," she said, showing me their website. "Allison said they usually list items there. If he dealt with Carrington and Cash on a regular basis, he might have some insight into their *real* working relationship."

"That feels like a bit of a long shot." Trouble was, at the moment we didn't have any short shots.

Dana shrugged. "Well, that's all I've got." She swiped the website closed and glanced at the time on her phone. "And I've gotta get going. I'm meeting Marco for menu planning. Oh, if Ricky ever asks, I told him I'm shoe shopping with you this afternoon." She gave me a wink.

* * *

There was an accident on Sepulveda, and it took nearly an hour to get back home. I just had time to tidy the house and run a couple of errands before it was time to pick the twins up from school. Luckily, after a long day of sandboxes and finger puppets, they were tired enough to go down for naps without too much of a protest. I'd just closed the bedroom door on the sweet sound of their gentle snoring when I heard Ramirez's car pull up outside. I glanced at the clock. Just past three. Way too early for my husband to be home. My stomach jumped up into my throat. That did not bode well.

Ramirez walked in the door and tossed his keys on the credenza with a distinct clatter.

"Hey, you," I said, crossing the room to give him a quick peck on the cheek.

"Hey, yourself," he returned.

"You're home early?" I phrased it in the form of a question.

He nodded. "Yeah."

Instead of elaborating, he stalked into the kitchen and grabbed a beer from the fridge. He popped the top and took a long swig.

Also not boding well.

I followed him into the kitchen, leaning tentatively against the counter. "So, any news on the Carrington case?" I almost hesitated to ask.

He took another swig. He took a deep breath. Then he leveled me with an unreadable look. "It's not looking good for your mom."

My stomach crawled from my throat to my chest, sitting with a hard thud. "How not good?"

He sighed, running a hand through his hair. "She's being considered as a suspect in Carrington's murder."

I shook my head. "No way. I mean, how can they possibly think she had anything to do with this?"

"The murder weapon belongs to her—"

"Lots of people are killed with stolen weapons," I protested.

"—and she has no solid alibi."

"She was only alone for a *couple* of minutes."

"Not to mention there were countless people at the *Extravaganza* who saw your mom cut loose on Carrington."

"*Before* he died," I protested. "No one actually saw my mom near Carrington when he was killed." I said it with certainty because I knew Mom was innocent. Though I was starting to feel like I was the only one.

Ramirez shook his head. "No, you're right. We don't have any positive ID on your mom. But honestly? The circumstantial evidence is pretty daunting against her."

"*Circumstantial*," I emphasized.

"For the moment."

"What does that mean?"

"It means that forensics is combing every inch of that venue for physical evidence to support the theory of the detectives in charge."

I pinched the bridge of my nose. "I take it *you* are not the detective in charge on this one?"

He shook his head. "No. Conflict of interest. Laurel and Hardy are lead on this one."

I closed my eyes and thought a really bad word. I'd run into Laurel McMartin and John Hardy before, and they had completely lived up to the buffoonery of their comical namesakes. How the two had ever made detectives, I had no idea. I had a feeling it had to do with greased palms, budget cuts, and a decline in the California school systems leading to overall lowered standards. And maybe the fact that Hardy's dad golfed with the commissioner.

"And their theory is that my mom killed Carrington?" I asked.

Ramirez took a step toward me, the hard look in his eyes softening. "I'm sorry, babe."

"But it's not true!" I shouted. "I know it looks bad, but you know my mom is innocent."

He nodded. "Of course I do."

"So convince them," I pleaded. "Tell them you know her. You know she didn't do it. It's just not in her character. She's being framed."

Ramirez sighed deeply again. "I'm afraid I'm not in a position to tell them anything.

"Why not?"

He gave me that sympathetic look again. "Because I've been pulled from the case."

Desperation made tears back up behind my eyes. "What?! Why?"

He reached out and pulled me in for a tight hug. "Sorry, Maddie," he murmured into my hair. "But if I were the captain, I'd have no choice but to pull me too. It's my mother-in-law. It's not like I can be impartial."

That's what I'd been counting on. As long as Ramirez was in there pulling for my mom, I thought she had a fighting chance of beating the stacked odds. She needed a partial party on her side. But if Laurel and Hardy were Mom's best bet at staying out of jail? Mom was in deep trouble.

CHAPTER FOUR

————

The next morning, my first destination—after getting the kids to preschool half an hour later because I'd had to comb the entire house for my cell phone, which I'd eventually found shoved into the crisper drawer of the refrigerator courtesy of Max the Phone Bandit—was my stepfather's salon, Fernando's of Beverly Hills. With circumstantial evidence mounting, I wanted to check in on Mom and see how she was holding up.

And as soon as I walked through the doors, that question was answered. Mom sat in the lobby, mascara streaking down her face in two long gray trails, her blue eye shadow smudged toward her hairline, and her hot pink lipstick half chewed away as she sobbed into a soggy tissue.

Beside her sat my stepfather, a comforting arm around her shoulders.

"What happened?" I asked, rushing to her side and placing a hand on her arm.

"The police were just here," Faux Dad explained, clucking his tongue. "Making"—he lowered his voice—"insinuations." His eyes went wide with infused meaning.

Faux Dad's real name was Ralph, he'd been born and raised in the Midwest, and his heritage was pure farm boy. But when he'd hit the West Coast and entered into a career coiffing the rich and famous, he'd had to reinvent himself to stand out. Hence, Fernando, stylist to the stars had been born. He'd gone full throttle with this new self, complete with a faux Spanish heritage, dyed black hair, and deep orange spray tans. In fact, I'd venture to say the only real thing about Faux Dad was his devotion to my mother.

"What did they say?" I asked, dread pooling in my belly.

"They're going to lock me up," Mom moaned into her tissue. "I'm going to the big house!"

I patted her back. "Mom, you're not going to the big house. I'm sure they're just asking questions."

"They were *interrogating* me. They think I'm g-g-guilty!" she wailed, breaking down into sobs again.

The bell at the front door jingled as Faux Dad's receptionist came bustling in.

"I got your text. I came as fast as I could," Marco said, tossing his yellow pleather shoulder bag onto the reception desk and making a beeline for Mom.

Marco was slim, Hispanic, and wore more eyeliner than Katy Perry. His pink sequined top sparkled above his black skinny jeans with tasteful holes ripped in the knees. He'd capped off the outfit with a pair of white boots with two-inch heels. (Which looked frighteningly like a pair I had in my own closet.) If Johnny Weir and J. Lo had a love child, it would be Marco.

"Two detectives just left," Faux Dad said, catching Marco up. "They were harassing Betty."

"I'm a s-s-suspect," Mom said, between sobs. She sniffed loudly. "I can't go to jail. Have you seen those mug shots? They're so unflattering. And I look terrible in orange!" She covered her face in the tissue again, blowing her nose loudly.

I patted her back some more as Marco tried to comfort her. "I'm sure it's just a formality. I mean, you both were at the scene of the crime," he said, looking to me. "Maybe you're just witnesses?"

Mom shook her head. "No. No they wanted my…alibi!" she wailed out.

I had to admit, that didn't sound good.

Faux Dad clicked his tongue again. "Look, I'm sure Ramirez will get to the bottom of this. He'll clear it up in no time."

I bit my lip. "Uh, maybe it would help if we went back over the timeline," I said, not ready to share yet that Ramirez was out of the loop in this one. "I mean, someone had to have gotten that hatpin from your purse, right?"

Mom sniffed and nodded, lifting her face. "I don't know how."

"Did you leave it alone at all?"

She looked at me like I'd suggested she'd slapped a puppy. "Leave my purse unattended? Why on earth would I do that?"

But I pressed forward. "Mom, if you didn't kill Carrington with that hatpin, someone else did, right?"

She nodded.

"So they must have taken it from your bag."

She nodded again, realization dawning that it could only *help* her to think of when she'd committed the cardinal sin of leaving a purse unattended. "But I'm afraid I had it with me all day."

"You didn't set it down? Like, even for a minute?"

She started to shake her head, but stopped. "Wait. I did set it down. But it was honestly just for a minute. I was eating a soft pretzel, and I was so frazzled from the fight with Carrington that I wasn't paying attention and a splotch of mustard dropped on my skort. Of course I'd forgotten to get napkins, and Dorothy was still getting her frozen lemonade, so I just popped up from my seat to grab a handful of napkins at one of the condiment kiosks. But honestly it couldn't have been more than a few seconds. A minute tops," she promised.

That was a mighty tight timeline, I had to agree. But it wasn't out of the realm of possibility that someone had been waiting for that very sort of opportunity. The hatpin would have been the last thing Mom had thrown into her purse. It would have been right on top. Honestly, it probably wouldn't have taken more than a couple of seconds to nab it.

"Did you notice anyone near you at the time?" I asked. Preferably lurking suspiciously.

Mom pursed her lips together, trying to think back. "Well, there was an older couple at the table next to me. And I remember seeing that lady with the clowns walk by."

"Clowns?" Marco asked.

"Ceramic clown dolls," I explained. "She was behind us in line." I turned to Mom. "And she knew Carrington, *and* you saw her at the food court too?" That was quite a coincidence, and I mentally put Clown Lady at the top of my suspect list.

Mom nodded. "Oh, and I remember a young man there too. He asked me if I knew where the coffee cart was." She perked up a bit. "In fact, I'd swear I saw him earlier when we were in Carrington's line too!"

Now we were getting somewhere. "Do you know who he is?" I asked.

She smiled. "Bradley Cooper."

I blinked. "Bradley Cooper?" I asked skeptically. What were the odds my mom was being framed by an Academy Award nominee?

She shook her head. "No, I mean not the real one. But the guy looked just like him. Spitting image." She sighed. "Kinda cute really."

Faux Dad cleared his throat.

"Oh, in a childish way, of course," Mom said, patting his hand. Then she turned back to me. "Does that help?"

She saw Clown Lady and a Bradley Cooper look-alike. I hated to say it, but this was far from a smoking gun. Still, it was something…

"Don't worry," I reassured her. "I'm sure we'll find out who really killed Carrington."

I only wished I was as confident as I sounded.

* * *

I left Mom in the care of Marco and Faux Dad and dialed Ramirez as I jumped back into my car. While Mom's info had been sparse, it was something.

"Ramirez," he answered on the third ring, obviously not checking the display.

"Hey, it's me," I said.

"Hey," he replied, his voice softer. "Everything okay?"

"Yeah. I was just with Mom."

He sighed. "How is she?"

"Been better." I paused. "Laurel and Hardy were here. They gave her quite a scare."

"Yeah, they scare me too," he mumbled. Though I knew that was for different reasons. "She okay?"

"She'll be fine," I said, hoping that was the truth. "I was wondering—have you seen the security camera footage from the *Antiques Extravaganza?*"

"Not yet. But, as you know, there were no cameras in the room where Carrington was found."

"Mom said she left her purse alone for just a minute while she grabbed some napkins in the food court. That must have been when the killer took the pin from Mom's purse."

"Okay. It's possible," Ramirez agreed on the other end.

"If they had cameras in the food court, maybe we could see who took it."

"I can check," Ramirez promised. "But from what I was told, the cameras were pretty strategically placed near the larger ticket items at the show. I doubt any were trained on the pretzel carts."

I felt my small hope bubble sink unceremoniously to the ground. "But it's worth a try?"

"I'll see what I can find," Ramirez promised. Though I had a feeling he already knew that the answer would be not much.

"Thanks," I told him.

"Hey, I gotta go. Love you," he said.

"Me too," I managed to get out before he hung up.

I stared down at my phone. If the security cameras were a bust, maybe I could get my hands on another camera that had been at the show that day. And I just happened to know one.

Cameron Dakota, the *L.A. Informer* paparazzo who had been popping off celebrity photos at the show.

I pulled up the number for the editor in chief of the tabloid, hesitating only briefly before dialing. To say Felix Dunn and I had a complicated history would be an understatement. At one point he'd been stalking me (for a story), and I'd punched him in the nose (for said stalking), and he'd kissed me, and I might have even kissed him back a little. In my defense, we'd been in a castle in England, and the romance had kind of swept me away. And, well, I might have had a few romantic feelings to begin with. Felix had a way of growing on people. Kind of like a fungus. In the end, I'd married Ramirez, Felix had started dating a reporter on his staff, and we'd found a way to peacefully coexist. Mostly by staying out of each other's lives.

I pushed the *Call* button and put it on speaker as I listened to the phone ring.

"Felix Dunn" came the response, in a deep British accent that immediately took me back in time to our *complicated* phase.

I cleared my throat. "Hey. It's, uh, Maddie."

The line went silent for a moment. "Maddie, what a surprise. How are you?"

"I've been better," I told him honestly.

"Oh?" His tone held sudden concern.

"Listen, long story short, Mom and I were at the *Antiques Extravaganza* when that appraiser, Carrington, was killed." I quickly filled him in about Mom's unfortunate hatpin incident.

"And the police think she did it?" he asked when I was finished.

"I'm afraid so."

"What about Ramirez?" he asked, his voice catching just a little on my husband's name.

"He's off the case."

"I'm sorry."

"Thanks." I paused. "But I'm not calling for sympathy. I, uh, need a favor."

"What sort of favor?" he asked.

"Cameron Dakota was at the show, right?"

"Yes," Felix responded slowly. I knew he protected his stories and sources like a mama bear protected her cubs. "Why?"

"I was just wondering if she might have caught any footage of the food court."

"Food court?" He sounded confused.

I quickly explained my theory that it was the only time someone could have taken the hatpin. "I was hoping she might have gotten a picture of someone near Mom at the time?" I didn't add that so far all I had were Bradley Cooper and clowns.

"I honestly couldn't tell you," he said. "She printed a few with her story last night, but I didn't see her entire roll."

"Would you mind if I took a look at it?"

"Be my guest," he agreed. "But Cam's out in the field right now. I can text you the address."

"Thanks," I said, finally feeling something go right today. "I owe you one."

"Be careful, Maddie," he said, his tone only half joking. "I may take you up on that someday."

CHAPTER FIVE

———

My GPS took me to the address Felix had given me, a sprawling house in Bel Air. The gated estate looked locked up tight, and there was no sign of Cameron or any other paparazzi outside. I drove past, noticing a construction site next door, where some lucky millionaire was getting a fully renovated mansion, and a couple more gated estates past that. I turned around in the cul-de-sac and drove past again, searching for any sign of Cam. Finally I parked on the street near the home under construction and got out, surveying the area on foot.

I was just about to give up and decide Felix had the wrong address, when I heard a female voice hail me from the foliage to my right.

"Psst. Maddie!"

I spun to find a construction worker peeking out from behind a row of Eucalyptus trees, a bright yellow helmet and orange reflective vest glinting in the sunlight.

"Cam?" I asked, moving toward the figure.

She lifted her hat as I approached and gave me a wide smile. "Felix told me you were on your way over."

"What's with the outfit?"

"I'm on a stakeout." I noticed she had a roll of papers tucked under her arm, her phone in one hand, and another hard hat in the other. She shoved the second yellow plastic helmet toward me. "Here. Put this on."

Vision of hat head danced before my eyes. "Uh, I'm good. I think I'll just—"

But Cam didn't wait for me to finish, unceremoniously placing it on my head. Which, considering she towered over me by a good six inches, was not a difficult feat for her. "I swiped it from the site manager's trailer. We're undercover. Walk with me."

Given little choice, I did, following her through the trees to the construction site. "Just keep your head down and don't make eye contact with anyone."

I nodded. "Okay. What are we doing here?"

"See that place?" She pointed toward the gated estate that had been the address Felix had provided.

"Yeah?"

"Brad Pitt is staying there."

I raised an eyebrow. "Looking to catch a candid shot?"

She nodded. "Yeah, especially since the house belongs to Jennifer Aniston."

"You think he's with her?" I had to admit, my inner tabloid reader perked up.

Cam's face broke into what could only be described as a giddy smile. "God, I hope so."

She led the way toward a pile of lumber and set the papers down, unrolling them to reveal a set of construction blueprints. She frowned, holding them up in the direction of the Aniston Love Shack, a look of concentration on her face.

"What are those?" I asked.

"Prop. They're of my aunt's condo in Manhattan Beach."

I stifled a laugh. "Nice."

"Hey, it's worked so far. I've been frowning at these blueprints for a couple hours now. No one wants to know why, or who might have screwed up, so they all leave me alone."

"Smart."

"Thanks." She paused, squinting at the windows of the house. A figure passed by one but disappeared just as quickly. "So Felix said you needed to see some pictures?"

I nodded under my heavy hat. "You were at the *Antiques Extravaganza*, right?"

Cam nodded. "I was. Who knew a puff piece on Charlize Theron's antique obsession was going to turn into a murder case?" Though, she didn't look entirely upset about it.

"That's sort of what I wanted to talk to you about." I gave her a brief rundown of my mom's involvement—or *non*involvement—in said murder and how someone must have taken the murder weapon from her purse at the food court.

"That's a short window of time," Cam said, eyes still on the house.

I nodded. "I know. But someone must have been watching my mom and waiting for the opportunity to grab the hatpin. I was hoping maybe I could take a look at the photos you shot at the *Extravaganza* to see if you might have caught anything useful from around that time?"

Cam gave me a sympathetic look. I was getting used to those these days.

"Sorry, but I don't think I shot anything at the food court. I was mostly on the convention floor, but you're welcome to look through the footage. It's all still on my camera."

She handed it to me, juggling the blueprints to pass it along.

"Just, keep the shutter open," she warned. "If I spot Pitt, I'm gonna need to catch him quickly."

I nodded. "Fair enough."

As Cam kept her eyes on the house next door, I pulled up the recent shots, scrolling through what seemed like hundreds of pictures taken in rapid succession of various parts of the convention center. Clearly Cam had wanted to have a few to choose from. The most recent were of the aftermath of the murder—CSI swarming, police corralling antiquers into tidy lines, EMTs huddled over Carrington's body. It was like watching the event unfold in reverse as I scrolled backward through shots. Unsettling at best, but nothing jumped out at me as particularly helpful to Mom's case.

Finally I found a shot of Carrington alive, which meant we were close to the timeline I was looking for.

Unfortunately, as Cam had said, nothing in her footage was near the food court. Shots of the line leading to Carrington, one photo of him with the Clown Lady as she shoved her jewel-buttoned toy in his direction. Lots of Charlize.

I was about to give up and hand the camera back, when something in the corner of one photo caught my eye. It was a picture of Carrington's line, but while the focus of the photos were the antiquers, I spied a figure just to the right, clad in all black, complete with a black pixie cut and pointy toed boots. Just like I'd seen his business partner wearing.

The business partner who said she hadn't been there.

"This woman," I said, showing her to Cam. "Do you have any more pictures of her?"

Cam took her eyes off the Love Shack long enough to study the figure, who, honestly, barely filled the corner of the frame, her face cut off. Cam shook her head slowly. "Sorry. I'm not sure. Who is she?"

"I'd bet money it's Carrington's business partner."

Cam gave me a blank look, like she was waiting for the punch line.

"I just talked to her yesterday, and she swore she wasn't at the *Extravaganza*."

Cam raised an eyebrow my way. "Well, that sounds suspicious, doesn't it?"

I grinned. "Very."

Cam took the camera from me and scrolled through a few photos. "If I had any more of that area, they'd be in this sequence." She paused, glancing at the Love Shack. "Keep an eye out for Pitt, would you?"

I nodded, keeping my gaze on the house as Cam scrolled. Well, mostly on the house. I couldn't help a little glance over her shoulder every now and then. Finally she straightened up and held the camera out toward me with a triumphant smirk. "Bingo."

I looked down at the view window. Carrington was behind his table, crouching down in a defensive position as my mom swung her purse toward his head. I cringed, but my embarrassment was short lived as I noticed the woman standing behind Carrington. At the time my attention had been focused on keeping Mom from beating the appraiser to death, but now I clearly saw Allison Cash just to the right of the commotion, her face front and center. There was no mistake about it. She had been there when Carrington was killed.

So why had she lied about it?

* * *

I left Cam frowning at her aunt's bathroom plumbing configurations as she waited for a Pitt/Aniston sighting, and jumped into my car. Before taking off, I pulled out my cell and dialed the number for Allison Cash's antique shop.

"Yesterday's Treasures. This is Mina. May I help you?"

"Hi, Mina. This is Maddie Springer," I said. "I was in your shop yesterday morning with the vintage Chanel heels."

"Right," Mina said. "I remember you. Did you change your mind about selling?"

"Uh, maybe," I hedged. "I was hoping to speak with Allison. Is she available?"

"I'm sorry, but she's not here right now."

"Can you tell me when she'll be in?" I asked.

"I'm not sure." Mina paused, as if unsure if she should share more. "She, uh, called in this morning saying she'd be out all day."

"Did she say why?" I pressed.

"Not exactly. But I think maybe Mr. Carrington's passing hit her pretty hard. I mean, they were close."

I jumped on the word. "Close? As in, they had a relationship?"

"Oh, no, nothing like that," Mina quickly backpedaled. "I just mean, they worked closely, you know? And, well, his death was so sudden. I think she just needs some personal time."

"Right," I said, only slightly deflated.

"I'm sure she'll be back in tomorrow."

"Tomorrow," I repeated. With the police hounding my mom, it sounded a million years away. I only hoped we had until tomorrow.

"Was there something maybe I could help you with?" Mina asked.

I shook my head in the empty interior of my car. "No. Thanks. But if you talk to Allison again, can you have her call me?" I left Mina with my number and thanked her before hanging up.

Allison had seemed anything but distraught yesterday over her partner's death. While it was possible emotion had hit her all at once today, it was also just as possible her sudden need for alone time was born out of guilt rather than grief.

Thinking of Dana's long-shot idea, I grabbed my phone and typed Van Steinberg's Auction House into my maps app. I still had my Chanel heels tucked away in my trunk, which felt like as good an excuse as any to visit them. If something had gone bad between the partners, I crossed my fingers that someone at the auction house knew something about it.

I pulled away from the curb and headed toward the freeway.

CHAPTER SIX

———

Two freeways, one overturned Prius, and forty-five minutes later I arrived at a large building in Century City. It was done in an ornate Mission Revival Style, with pale taupe stucco walls, adobe inspired arches and colonnades, and intricately carved dormers and niches. A small parking lot sat in the back and, thankfully, was largely empty at the moment. I slid into a spot near the entrance, grabbed my shoebox from the back, and made my way inside.

While the styling was nineteenth century, the plush carpeting, cool air conditioning, and bright LED lighting said the amenities were all modern. The air held the same reverence and loftiness I'd associate with a museum, and I instinctually felt myself wanting to use my indoor voice as I approached a large walnut reception desk.

"May I help you?" asked the woman in glasses behind the desk.

"Yes. I was hoping to speak to someone about putting these vintage shoes in an auction?" I said, phrasing it as a question. To be honest, all the auction experience I had was on eBay. This was a little out of my league, and I wasn't sure what to expect.

She sent me a pleasant smile. "First time here?"

I nodded.

"Let me get Mr. Van Steinberg. He can give you a better idea about if we're the right place for your item." While it was said in the same pleasant voice, I suddenly felt like my shoes were under scrutiny, and I hoped they'd pass muster.

I waited a beat while the woman disappeared into a back office, and a moment later she emerged with an older man in an impeccably tailored suit with strategic creases in all the right places. His face was tanned, his white goatee trimmed neatly, and as he offered his hand in greeting, I noticed his nails were perfectly manicured. He seemed the type that crumbs wouldn't dare adhere to. I self-consciously brushed at my own skirt, hoping it didn't hold any lingering goldfish dust.

"Richard Van Steinberg," he told me, shaking my hand. "You have an item you'd like to auction?"

"Maddie Springer," I offered. "And yes. I was hoping to learn a little bit more about my vintage shoes. Chanel." I patted the box and smiled. "And maybe put them up for auction."

"Please step into my office, and we'll have a look at them." He gestured to the back, and I followed his lead, coming into a large room that looked like a Victorian library straight off the *Downton Abby* set. High backed chairs, tufted loveseat, carved wooden bookcases filled with leather volumes and stained glass lamps, and a variety of oil paintings on the walls. Richard stood behind a walnut desk that looked like the granddaddy of the one in the reception room, and he indicated a pair of leather chairs in front for me before taking his seat.

I sat and slid the box across the desk. He opened it slowly, with the appropriate reverences the items deserved, and removed one pump. "These are in very nice condition," he said, giving me an approving look. "Looks like a '62 or '63. Kitten heel, sling-back." He looked up at me. "Any idea what you're looking to get out of them?"

"Honestly, I'm not sure," I admitted. "I took them to the *Antiques Extravaganza* to get an idea what they were worth, but I never got a chance to get them appraised."

At the mention of the show, Van Steinberg's face darkened. "Yes. Nasty business, that."

"Were you at the show?"

He nodded. "Briefly. We tend to get an influx of people wanting to sell their items at auction after a show like that comes through town."

"Having found out how much Grandma's ugly pottery is really worth," I surmised.

He gave me a wry smile. "Exactly. I like to browse the show ahead of time and see if anything really stunning makes an appearance." He frowned. "Only, I didn't get much of a chance this time."

"Did you know Carrington?" I asked.

He nodded. "Yes. The antiques community is a small one."

"I'm very sorry for your loss," I told him.

He looked momentarily surprised, as if the thought he should be upset by the death hadn't yet occurred to him. "Uh, yes, well, thank you."

"Were the two of you close?"

Van Steinberg let out a bark of laughter. "Hardly."

Now we were getting somewhere. "Oh. Why is that?"

He leveled me with a look. "I don't wish to speak ill of the dead."

Though, with that sentence he kinda already had. "I take it you were not a fan of his?"

"Oh, Carrington had enough fans. Every flea-market Sally who saw him on TV suddenly started showing up at our auctions."

"I would think that would be good for business."

"Sure. *If* they ever bought anything. But they just came to look and get close to Carrington. Antique groupies, if you will." He shook his head.

I thought of the Clown Lady and how she'd practically fawned over him as we'd stood in line at the show. "I think I met one of them at the *Extravaganza*. Petite, dark bob, glasses. Has a thing for clowns."

"Ah." He nodded. "Yes, I've seen her here several times. Never buys," he added, scowling.

"I don't suppose you have a name for her?"

He shook his head. "I wouldn't know."

"What about Carrington's partner?" I asked, switching gears. "Allison Cash?"

"What about her?" he asked. If he had any opinion of her, it didn't show, his expression remaining neutral. His eyes were on the shoes again, examining a microscopic bit of something on the toe.

"Do you work with her regularly as well?"

"I'm sure she's been in once or twice. But I believe she handled more of the business aspects and Carrington did more of the hands-on appraisals and auctions."

"Did *they* get along?" I asked.

Again Carrington's eyes went to mine, this time narrowing ever so slightly. In his defense, it was an odd question for someone looking to auction a pair of shoes.

"I, uh, just ask because Allison seemed to lowball me when I had these in her shop yesterday. Just wondering if she was always that difficult or…" I let the thought trail off. Admittedly, it was a lame excuse.

But he seemed to buy it, as he shrugged. "I wouldn't take it personally. Like I said, Allison was the business brain behind the operation. She was probably just looking out for her bottom line."

Which didn't tell me anything about how the partners got along.

I decided to try a different tactic. "The police are saying Carrington was murdered."

"Hmm," Van Steinberg mumbled. "Yes, I heard that."

"Do you know if Carrington had problems with anyone? Any disputes with clients or other dealers?"

Van Steinberg snorted. "Knowing Carrington? He likely had problems with everyone."

This guy really wasn't a fan. I wondered if there was a specific reason Van Steinberg didn't like Carrington or just a general distaste toward the man.

"Had Carrington auctioned anything here recently?" I asked. I was fishing, but you never knew when a shark might bite your line.

"Well, let me see." His forehead wrinkled in concentration. "I believe the last two items he brought in both sold at our previous auction. A Veldenshort oil on canvas and a Bracington sculpture." He paused. "From the Heffernan Studios."

"I'm familiar with the style," I mumbled, remembering The Blob Lottie LaMore had been peddling.

"Oh, a modern art fan?"

"Isn't everyone?" I gave him a bright smile, hoping he bought it. "When was it you said the last piece sold?"

"Last month. The Bracington sculpture. Buyer was anonymous."

I frowned. "Anonymous? Then how do you know who takes the item home?"

"It was bought through a broker. He handles the transaction, and the buyer compensates him. Usually a small percentage."

"I had no idea," I mused. This was much more involved than eBay.

"With some of our higher dollar items, buyers prefer that the ownership not be of public record." He shot me a knowing look. "Tax purposes and all that."

I nodded, pretending to understand the issues of the 1%.

"I'll admit, I've never brought an item to an auction house before. How does the process work?" I asked, genuinely curious.

He studied the bottom of a heel, then sat the shoe back in the box.

"It's going to vary depending on what you're auctioning. We have formal auctions here on site every month. We generally fill them at least two to three months ahead of time."

"Oh, I didn't realize," I mumbled.

He waved a hand. "For the larger ticket items. We need the time to photograph items, prepare brochures, and promote the auction. For items like that we do sometimes charge storage and insurance fees as well, but again we're talking bigger ticket pieces. For an item like these," he said, gesturing to the heels, "we can usually fit them in as an add-on piece. Or, quite honestly, I think they'd do well at one of our day auctions."

"Day auctions?" I asked. "What are those?"

"Well, often our marquee auctions are in the evening, many of them invitation only."

Sounded exclusive. And expensive.

"But," he went on, "we usually have a more informal auction the day after to sell off smaller items or those that didn't find a buyer the previous evening. Starting bids and buyers' premiums are generally lower, and they're open to the public. In fact we have one of those scheduled for tomorrow."

"And you think these might be a good fit for a day auction?"

He nodded. "I do. These shoes are in quite good condition, with the exception of a little wear on the heels here." He lifted a shoe and pointed to the bottom for me to take a look. "I'd say you could expect in the neighborhood of two to three hundred dollars for them. Possibly more if the right buyer is interested."

Which was far more than Allison Cash had offered. "And what fees would I owe?"

"Just a sales commission. For these, let's say 10%."

The truth was, it had been years since I'd worn the Chanel. As much as I loved owning a part of fashion history, they'd seen more of my closet than strutting down Rodeo. I'd enjoyed them, and the idea of giving them a new home with someone else who could appreciate them was enticing. Especially if it meant a couple hundred in my pocket and an invitation to delve deeper into Peter Carrington's world.

I stuck my hand out toward the pristine man. "You've got a deal."

CHAPTER SEVEN

———

After filling out some paperwork and leaving my Chanel heels in Van Steinberg's care, I got back into my car and hit a drive-thru Starbucks, contemplating my next move. Van Steinberg had given me precious little to go on about Allison Cash other than she was the businesswoman behind Carrington's TV face. And while it was clear the auctioneer didn't have a very high opinion of Carrington himself, I didn't see him killing the guy over a few groupies. His reaction hadn't been any worse than anyone else in Carrington's life to the news of his demise. In fact, so far no one I'd encountered actually seemed to have liked the guy very much...with the possible exception of Clown Lady. Who *had* been at the show when Carrington was killed and *had* gotten a front row seat to Mom's altercation with him. While I wasn't sure of motive, Clown Lady definitely had opportunity and means to off the appraiser.

I took a cooling sip of my Frappuccino and set it in my cup holder, making a sharp right onto Santa Monica, heading back toward Venice. If Clown Lady had been a regular at Van Steinberg's auctions, chances were she'd frequented Yesterday's Treasures as well. And it was quite possible friendly Mina had thought to ask for a name where impersonal Van Steinberg had not.

I was just indulging in the last syrupy sips of my coffee concoction when I parked in front of the antique shop. Through the window I could see more bodies filling the shop today than there had been yesterday. However, as I pushed through the glass doors, I realized the bodies were not patrons but police. Laurel and Hardy to be specific.

I paused, ducking my head away from the two, lest they recognized me, and feigning interest in the jewelry case to their left. (Which wasn't really all that hard, as it was an interesting case!)

John Hardy had a generous amount of padding in the middle and a 1990s soul patch on his stumpy chin. His dress shirt was wrinkled and had a suspicious-looking brown stain near the pocket, his slacks were at least an inch too long, pooling unflatteringly around his ankles, and he'd capped off his plainclothes not-so-chic outfit with a dark fedora that looked more Halloween costume quality than Sinatra sultry. In contrast to Hardy's disheveled self, Laurel McMartin was buttoned up, pressed, and starched to within an inch of her life. Her dark hair was pulled back from her face in a ponytail so tight that it made her makeup-less eyes slant upward. She wore dark slacks that were just a little too tight on the rear and a little too loose in the legs, a pale blue dress shirt, and sensible low heeled black loafers.

They each had their smartphones out, consulting what I assumed to be notes as they questioned Mina—who was minus the smile today, standing behind the counter and chewing on an unpainted fingernail as her eyes darted from one detective to the other.

"So you were here the day of the *Antiques Extravaganza*?" Laurel said.

Mina nodded. "That's right."

"Not at the show?" Hardy asked.

Mina shook her head.

"Alone?" he pressed.

"Uh…I guess. I mean some customers came in…"

"Got names for them?" Laurel demanded.

"I guess I could check our receipts, but not everyone who came in bought something."

"Yeah, we'll need to see those," Laurel told her, glancing down at her phone screen to type some notes.

"Uh, okay. I'll have to ask Ms. Cash…"

"That would be Alexis Cash?" Hardy asked, squinting at the screen of his own phone.

"Allison Cash," Mina corrected.

Hardy shot her a sharp look. "I have Alexis."

Mina shook her head. "It's Allison."

Hardy turned to his partner. "What do you have?"

"I've got…" Laurel held the phone out at arm's length, eyes narrowing at the screen. "Alejandro?"

Hardy shot an accusatory look at Mina. "Okay, so which is it?"

"Allison?" Mina said, though her voice held a note of question.

"Huh." Hardy looked back at his notes. "It's the damned autocorrect," he told Laurel. "Does yours have autocorrect?"

"You have to turn that off."

"You can turn it off?"

"Yeah, you go to settings, then… Oh, just let me do it." She grabbed Hardy's phone.

"What's that screen? I've never seen that screen before."

"Well, your settings are different than mine…"

I wasn't sure if I should laugh or cry that my mom's fate was in the hands of these two.

"There," Laurel finally said. "It's off."

"So, how come yours did 'Alejandro'?"

"Oh, well, I was using speech to text."

"You can do that?"

"Yeah. Just push this little icon—"

"Um, was there anything else?" Mina asked, looking antsy.

Hardy turned back to her as if suddenly remembering where he was. "Yeah, as a matter of fact, there is. We'd like to speak to Al—er, your boss."

"She's not in," Mina said, "She's taking a personal day."

"Personal day, huh?" Laurel said, making a note on her phone.

"Yes. She was distraught," Mina explained, sounding defensive.

"I bet she was." Hardy shot Laurel a knowing look.

Laurel smirked back.

"She was," Mina protested. She paused. "Why did you need to speak with her?"

"We need to follow up with her about a tip we received," Hardy told her.

My ears perked up, and I nudged myself a little closer to the pair.

"Tip?" Mina asked.

Laurel nodded. "About fake antiques."

Mina frowned. "What about them?"

"You ever sell any?"

"Wh-what?" Mina took a step back from the counter. "No. Of course not!"

"You sure about that?" Hardy asked, leaning his pudgy elbows on the counter.

"Yes!" She frowned. "Every item we sell has been authenticated, if not by a certifying agency, then by one of our owners."

"So they say," Laurel said, pointedly.

But Mina shook her head. "No, there's no way they would do that. Who told you we were selling fakes?"

"Sorry, we can't divulge our sources," Laurel told her.

"Well, whoever it was, they are wrong."

Laurel gave Hardy a look. Hardy smirked this time. Laurel wrote something down.

"Have your boss call us when she gets in, huh?" Hardy told Mina, shoving a business card across the counter at her.

Mina pursed her lips but didn't answer as she watched Laurel and Hardy leave the shop.

I gave her a two count to compose herself again while I digested the information that *CSI: Dumb and Dumber Edition* had just dropped. Had someone accused Carrington of selling fake antiques? If he'd been scamming clients, that lent itself nicely to a motive to want him dead. Especially if someone had paid top dollar for said fake, I decided, thinking of the two items Carrington had sold at Van Steinberg's auction before he died.

I cleared my throat and approached Mina.

She tore her gaze from the front doors, noticing me for the first time. "Oh, sorry. Can I help you?"

I smiled at her, trying to ease some of the tension the Laurel and Hardy act had set into her shoulders. "I was in here yesterday. With the Chanel shoes?"

"Oh, right." Mina's posture relaxed a bit as recognition dawned.

"Maddie," I offered.

"Right. How can I help you, Maddie?"

"I take it Allison is still out?"

She nodded. "Unfortunately." She glanced back toward the glass door, outside which I could clearly see Laurel making more adjustments to Hardy's phone, Hardy gesturing wildly with his arms as he tried to explain his technology woes.

"Everything okay?" I asked, even though I'd eavesdropped on most of the conversation.

She blew out sigh. "Yeah. They're detectives. Looking into Carrington's murder."

"They have any leads?" I asked, not sure I wanted to hear the answer.

Mina shrugged. "They just asked a ton of questions I wasn't sure how to answer."

"Oh? Like what?" I asked, trying my best to sound casual.

"They just showed me some pictures of this older woman and asked if I'd ever seen her in the shop, if Carrington knew her, if she had anything against Carrington."

I felt my chest tighten. "The older woman...she didn't happen to have a whole lot of blue eye shadow and kind of '80s style clothes, did she?"

Mina nodded. "Yeah. Why?"

I sighed. "I, uh, might have seen the same pictures."

"Yeah, well, they seemed pretty sure she did it. And then they accused us..." She paused, biting her lip.

I nodded sympathetically. "I overheard about the fake antiques."

"Well, it's not true!" she said hotly. "Honestly, I don't know who told them that, but Carrington would never do such a thing. Can you imagine what that would do to our reputation? I guess they thought he sold a fake item to this woman and she lost it on him."

As far as I knew, Mom had never set foot in Yesterday's Treasures. But I wasn't sure a little thing like actual evidence was going to stop Laurel and Hardy.

"Anyway, was there something I could help you with?"

"Actually, I think there might be," I said. "I met a woman at the *Antiques Extravaganza* the other day," I began. "She had this little clown doll. I didn't catch her name, and I was wondering if you might happen to know who she was. I got the feeling she was a big fan of Carrington's."

"Ah. Yeah, that would be Terri Voy. She's in here all the time. Always with clowns. They're kind of her thing, I guess." She shrugged, as if she didn't get it either.

"So she knew Carrington well?"

Mina shrugged. "She came to see him a lot, but I don't know if they were friends or she was just a fan or what. She never really wanted to chat with me—just asked for Carrington." Mina paused. "Why do you ask? Did you want to buy one of her clowns?"

I tried not to visibly shudder at the thought. "Uh, yeah," I lied. "I might. You don't happen to have her address, do you?"

Mina pursed her lips and shook her head. "Sorry. We don't keep info like that. If Mr. Carrington did, it would be on his computer. Which they already took." She nodded in the direction of the detectives, who were both looking at their screens now, squinting and comparing.

I thanked Mina and left, telling her again to pass on my message to Allison Cash when she came in.

* * *

As soon as I hopped back into the car, I pulled up my trusty friend Google and typed in *Terri Voy*. In addition to finding a social media page covered in clown-themed skins and a small article on a collector's blog about the rising popularity of porcelain clowns, I found a White Pages listing with an address in Pasadena. I checked my dash clock. I only had an hour before I had to pick up the twins. Possibly enough time to question Terri about her groupie status with the deceased, but I'd be cutting it close to get back across town in time. I decided not to chance it (I swear it had nothing to do with a fear of clowns—strictly a timeline thing) and instead did a quick drive-thru Del Taco run before picking up the tiny twosome.

Happily sated with french fries and tacos in their matching car seats, the twins giggled in the back while I headed toward home. I'd only gotten a couple of blocks, however, when my Bluetooth rang with a call from Marco.

"What's up?" I asked.

"Maddie, thank gawd you're free!" came Marco's voice through my car speakers.

"I'm not exactly free…" I hedged, glancing in the rearview at the kids (throwing shredded cheese at each other). "I'm in the car—"

"We have a situation," Marco said, plowing ahead.

My mind immediately went to Mom. "Is everything okay? What kind of situation?"

"A terrible one," I heard Dana's voice come over the line.

"Dana, is that you? What's going on?"

"I'm about to fire my party planner, is what's going on!"

I heard a gasp and a whimper. "You wouldn't dare."

"Watch me," Dana argued.

"What's wrong?" I cut in, relieved that whatever the *situation* was, it had nothing to do with Mom. "Where are you guys?"

"That is the problem!" Dana answered. "I'm in Watts standing in front of a warehouse called *Borrow a Burro*."

"Excuse me?" I asked, slightly distracted by the food fight going on in the backseat as lettuce became weaponized.

"She's being dramatic. We're only on the *border* of Watts," Marco said back, clearly missing the horrifying part of the last statement.

"Give me that," I heard Dana say to Marco before her voice came back to me, louder this time, as if she'd gained control of the speaker phone. "I'm standing in front of a place called Borrow a Burro, where my illustrious party planner says we're…"

"Borrowing burros?" I guessed, trying hard to hide my snicker.

"This is not funny!"

I guess I didn't try hard enough.

"Help me, Maddie!" she pleaded.

I heard scuffling, then Marco's voice as he took the phone back. "Let me explain," he said.

"Please do." I made a left onto Pico as a hunk of chicken sailed past my head.

"So we may possibly have had a slight wrinkle in Ricky's party plans."

"Slight?!" I heard Dana yell in the background.

"It all started with camels," he went on, ignoring her. "Okay, so know how Oprah had her guests taken into that hot party on the backs of camels? Oh, so Arabian Nights chic," he sighed, apparently internally swooning just thinking about a party with Oprah.

"Go on," I prompted, reaching into the backseat with one hand to take away Max's juice box, which he'd started using as a firehose on his sister.

"Well, turns out camels are against the city ordinance. Go figure! You need, like, all these permits and stuff." He huffed at the indignity of it.

"Can you believe it, Maddie?" Dana cut in. "He wants to use camels to transport Ricky's birthday party guests!"

"No, no, no," Marco said. "Are you not listening? No camels. That's the problem."

"How about the guests just walk in?" I suggested.

Marco gasped. "You're joking?"

I rolled my eyes. Luckily no one saw it but the twins.

"Anyway, I came up with the *perfect* solution," Marco continued, emphasizing the word.

"Let me guess," I said. "Borrowing a burro?"

"Exactly! You see, burros are small enough to skirt the need for permits. They're perfect! Genius, right?"

"My guests are not riding donkeys!" Dana cried.

"Not ride," Marco said. "Experience. It's a whole experience!"

"A stinky, dirty, experience," Dana cut in.

"Rustic. Unique." He paused. "Besides, they'll go great with the flock of peacocks I rented."

"Peacocks!" Dana yelled.

"What? You said we needed color."

"I meant flowers. Balloons."

"You should have been more specific, dahling. And we can't do balloons. They'll scare the burros."

I heard Dana make a growling sound, followed by an impassioned plea of, "Maddie, help!"

"Yes, what do you think, Maddie?" Marco pleaded.

Suddenly there was silence on the other end of the line for the first time since I'd made the mistake of taking this call.

"Oh, me? Well, gee, I don't know..." I trailed off. Honestly? The idea of burro riding was not my fave. But taking sides could only end one way—with one pouty friend.

"I know you don't want to ride a filthy donkey in a cute little party dress and heels," Dana said, trying to sway me to her side.

"Burro!" Marco corrected. "And they're in the top ten cleanest-animals-of-all-time list."

"According to whom?" Dana demanded.

"I-I read it somewhere."

"Lemme guess, the Borrow a Burro brochure?" she said, heavy on the sarcasm.

"Gee, wish I could help," I started, feeling my nose grow at the lie, "but I'm just hitting Laurel Canyon. I'm about to lose you."

"But, Maddie," Marco protested.

"Sorry, I..." I paused, hoping it sounded like my phone cutting out.

"Mads?" Dana called.

"...breaking up...call you later...gotta go..."

And I hung up.

I felt a teeny tiny bit guilty as I made a right *not* on Laurel Canyon to drive through the notoriously spotty cell service of the Hollywood Hills, but onto my own street in a well-appointed service area of West LA. I spun around in my seat, addressing the taco warriors in the back.

"Never lie," I told them. "Unless it's to save a friendship from a battle over burros."

Livvie giggled. Max threw the last of his cheese at me.

* * *

After bathing both twins, quickly showering the taco seasoning off myself, and thoroughly vacuuming out my car while the twins built a Duplo tower in the living room, I was just pouring myself a much needed glass of wine when I heard Ramirez's car pull into the driveway. A few beats later, his frame filled the kitchen doorway.

"Hey you," I said, raising my glass in greeting. "You're home early again."

He crossed the room and kissed me on the forehead. "Slow day at the office."

"I'm gonna take that as a good thing in this case."

He shot me a wry smile as he opened the fridge, coming out with a beer in hand. "What's that smell? Burritos?"

Guess I should have taken a little more time in the shower. "I got the twins Del Taco after school."

He raised an eyebrow my way. "Save me any?"

I nodded toward a brown paper bag on the counter. "Two chicken soft tacos with extra Del Scorcho sauce."

"Have I told you lately how much I love you?" he asked, digging in.

I grinned. "Tell me with some good news. Any developments on Carrington's murder?"

He paused mid-bite. "Developments? Yes. Good news? Not so much."

I groaned. "What happened?"

"Well, we got forensics info back today." He ripped open a packet of hot sauce with his teeth, dumping a generous amount on his taco.

"Mom's not in jail, is she?"

He grinned. "I think you would have heard by now."

I took a fortifying sip of rosé. "Okay, hit me. What is it?"

Ramirez sighed. "Prints came back on the murder weapon."

"You got prints off a pin?" I was impressed.

He nodded. "A partial on the back of the gem housing."

"And?"

"And it's a match for your mom."

"Well, of course it is," I said, gesturing in the air with my hands. "It's *her* hatpin."

"Hers was the only print."

"So, the killer wore gloves," I told him. "He could do that, right?"

Ramirez pinned me with a look. "Or she."

I set my glass down. "My mom did *not* kill Carrington."

Ramirez blew out another sigh. "*I* know that. And *you* know that."

"But Laurel and Hardy don't know that," I finished his thought.

Ramirez nodded. "Sorry, babe. But the evidence isn't looking good."

I grabbed the wineglass and took another healthy swig. "Anything else come back from forensics?"

Ramirez sipped his beer. "Just that the victim was stabbed from behind, so with the element of surprise, it wouldn't have taken much strength to kill him."

"Meaning even a woman like my mom could have done it." I felt the wine suddenly burning a hole through my stomach.

"Sorry," Ramirez said again, pulling me in for a hug.

I reveled in the warmth for a moment before I told him, "I ran into Laurel and Hardy today."

"Oh?" he stepped back, grabbing his taco again. "How did that go?"

I quickly filled him in on my day, including the trip to the auction house and the scene I'd witnessed at the antique shop. "Mina swore the antiques they sold were real, but I've been wondering."

"That's never good." Ramirez shot me a grin.

I gave him a playful swat on the arm. "What if the anonymous tip was right? What if Carrington actually was selling fakes, and someone found out and killed him over it?"

"You're thinking a duped customer?"

"Or auction house owner," I added, thinking of Van Steinberg and his vocally low opinion of Carrington. "What if Carrington put a fake into an auction, the person who won it found out, and he came back to Van Steinberg with it?"

"I can't imagine Van Steinberg would be too happy about it."

I nodded. "No. Unhappy enough to kill even."

"Possibly," Ramirez said, playing devil's advocate. "But *maybe* fakes and *possible* anger aren't evidence, babe."

He was right. While it was a nice theory, that was all it was. It hardly stacked up against fingerprints and eyewitnesses to Mom calling Carrington every name in the book.

"There's also the clown lady," I added.

Ramirez choked on his bite of taco. "You've got a theory about a clown?"

I shook my head. "She's not a clown. She just collects them."

"That's better?"

"Barely?" I chuckled. "Anyway, it seems she was a bit of a fan of Carrington's. She showed up at the antiques shop and Carrington's auctions. She was actually behind us in line to see Carrington at the *Extravaganza*, so I know she had opportunity."

He nodded. "Motive?"

He had me there. "I'm working on that," I mumbled, lifting my glass to my lips.

"Don't worry, babe," he said, patting me on the back. "Look, we both know that your mom is innocent, so the evidence will point that way eventually."

I just hoped eventually came before Laurel and Hardy made an arrest.

CHAPTER EIGHT

———

When Ramirez and I had been just dating, I'd had my backside grabbed by a drunk clown at a child's birthday party, which had ended in my future husband slugging the guy, and me with a face full of birthday cake. Last year, just before the twins' first birthday, I'd had a clown set fire to my living room in a botched juggling incident that had ended in the death of Ramirez's favorite recliner. Both incidents had contributed to my dislike of clowns, and that dislike was only growing the longer I sat in Terri Voy's living room the following morning.

Display cases full of porcelain clown figurines and soft-bodied dolls lined the far wall. Paintings of sad clowns, happy clowns, and scary clowns hung on the opposite one. A sequined throw pillow with a clown's face sat on the armchair, next to a woven throw blanket adorned with an entire circus scene. On the wooden coffee table in front of me was a vase in the shape of a clown, with its hand holding the bouquet of dried flowers. Next to a coffee table book on—what else?—clowns. Everywhere I looked, a pair of inanimate eyes stared at me over a round red nose.

I licked my lips, infinitely glad I'd enlisted Dana to come as backup. If I'd been alone, I might have bolted at the door. As it was, I took a deep breath, steeled my strength, and turned to the petite woman sitting on the sofa across from me.

"Wow, this is some collection," I told her.

"Thanks." Terri Voy smiled shyly. "I adore clowns." She smiled affectionately at a small doll sitting on the sofa beside her. "They are just so lively."

If any of these started getting lively, I was out of there. "Uh-huh," I agreed.

"So, you mentioned you want to talk to me about Peter. Are you with the police?" Terri asked.

I nodded. "Sort of." Okay, that was *sort of* a lie. But there were all definitions of "with." I was married to a police officer, so I was kind of "with" him, right?

"And you knew Peter?" Terri asked, adjusting her glasses on her nose.

"We met briefly," I told her. "At the *Antiques Extravaganza.*"

"Right." She nodded, her dark bob bouncing up and down as recognition dawned. "I remember you. Your mom was the one who got in that argument with Peter."

I cleared my throat. "Yes, but she feels bad about that now."

"It's okay. Peter was sometimes hard to get along with like that."

"Really?" Dana leaned forward. "There were other people he argued with recently?"

Terri blinked at me behind her large glasses. "Oh, no. I mean, I didn't mean that. It's just he was…well, appraisal is an art form. And like any artist, he had that passion in him." She picked up the doll beside her, cradling it in her lap for comfort. "Sorry. I'm still a bit in shock." Her voice broke on the last word, showing the first signs of genuine emotion at Carrington's death that I'd encountered.

"I'm sorry," I said. "Were you close?"

Terri nodded her head. "Very." She blew out a sigh and looked up again, her eyes watering behind the glass magnification. "We were in love."

That was as surprise. "You and Carrington?"

She nodded solemnly. "Yes."

I frowned, thinking back to how Mina had said Carrington was single. "How long had you been dating him?"

"Oh." Terri blushed. "No, we weren't dating. I mean, we hadn't been on a formal date. Not really. Unless you counted all the time we'd spent together at auctions and shows. But we were in love."

I was beginning to get a clearer picture. "Did Carrington know you were in love?" I asked slowly.

Her eyes shot to mine. "Of course he did! I know he loved me!" She paused, looking from me to Dana. "He-he just never got the chance to say it."

I glanced at Dana and could see my thoughts mirrored in her expression—the adoration sounded kinda one-sided.

"Look I know what you're thinking," Terri said.

Was my poker face that bad?

"What would a god like Carrington be doing with me," she supplied, the blush deepening.

"I wasn't thinking that at all," I told her honestly.

"But he loved me. And he would have told me so too. Much sooner if *she* hadn't come along."

"She?" Dana asked.

Terri's expression darkened. "Allison." She spit the word out like it tasted sour. "She was poisoning him."

"Poison?" Dana perked up.

"With her evil spirit."

Dana's shoulders slumped. "Oh. Right."

"I take it you weren't a fan of Allison?" I asked Terri.

"Look, everything was fine before she came along. Then as soon as he started working with her, he was suddenly cold to me. Distant. I know it was her doing!" Her voice rose, and I swore her glasses were starting to fog up.

I could easily see her going from docile fan to crazy stalker.

"Did Carrington ever say anything about her?" Dana asked.

Terri got her breath under control, shaking her head. "No, but I hadn't been able to get him alone lately."

"Is that why you were at the *Extravaganza*?" I asked.

She nodded and twisted the little clown doll over in her hands. "Yes. I was there to see him. Look, he was busy with the TV show lately, doing more appraisals and traveling, and it was getting harder and harder to catch him at the store. Usually it was just that awful woman and the shopgirl there. And every time I tried to talk to him at the auction house, he was busy with a client. I mean, it was almost like he was avoiding me!"

Go figure.

"Anyway, I just thought if I could get him alone for a few minutes, he'd see what a mistake he was making. He'd see how right we were for each other. How much he loved me." She paused. "And not her."

"Allison?" I asked.

"Yes." She sat the clown down hard on the sofa, as if it were the toy's fault. "She wouldn't let me talk to him. She did it on purpose! She'd just shoo me away. Like I was nothing! I wasn't nothing to Peter!"

"Did you talk to Carrington at the show?" I asked. She had been right behind us in line, so she must have gotten to him before the killer did. Assuming they were not one and the same.

Terri's eyes watered again. "Yes. But he was too busy to talk about us. He loved my clown though." Her voice broke on the last word, tears trickling down her cheeks.

"When Carrington was killed, where were you?" I asked, liking my crazy stalker theory more and more.

Terri whipped her bob my way. "What do you mean?"

"I was just wondering if you were close enough to Peter to have seen anything helpful," I lied.

"Oh. Well, no. I guess not." She sniffed loudly. "After he looked at my clown, I decided to browse the Toys line to see if anyone had brought a Brunoro." She paused. "That's a collectible clown maker from Italy."

I nodded, as if I was noting that down.

"Anyway, I'm afraid I was on the other side of the convention floor when Peter…when it happened," she finished quietly.

Which was a convenient alibi, but without security cameras to back her up, it was just her word.

The same as Mom's.

* * *

As soon as we got back to the car, I started the engine and blasted the air conditioner.

"That place was creepy," Dana said. "Did you see all those little eyes on us?"

I nodded, looking across the street at Terri's place, almost expecting a *lively* doll to be staring back at us through the window. "What do we think about her story?"

"I think she's nuts," Dana said, not pulling any punches.

"The tears seemed real enough," I mused, almost feeling sorry for her.

Pft. Dana blew a disbelieving puff of air between her lips. "I can cry on cue like that."

"You really think she was faking?" I asked.

Dana shrugged. "Or not. Maybe she had a crazy love obsession thing for him, killed him when she realized he didn't love her, and now she's actually sad and missing him."

"Sounds like a Lifetime movie," I mumbled.

Dana nodded. "Yeah, I think I auditioned for that one once. Nailed the cry-on-cue part." She winked at me.

I laughed. "Okay, well, what about Allison Cash?"

"What about her?" Dana asked, popping a stick of gum into her mouth.

"Do you think she was really purposely trying to keep Terri away from Carrington?"

Dana chewed, squinting into space as she thought about that. "Maybe. Maybe it was just Terri's warped imagination."

"You're awfully hard on her," I said.

Dana shot me a look. "Did you hear her flimsy alibi?"

I had. And I agreed. "But Allison Cash lied about being at the *Antiques Extravaganza.* Why would an innocent person do that?"

Dana shrugged. "You got me there." She paused. "Have you talked to Allison?"

I shook my head as I put the car in gear and pulled away from the curb. "I tried, but she was taking a personal day yesterday."

"Hmm," Dana said. "Maybe today is the day."

*   *   *

Dana had an appointment with the caterer for Ricky's surprise party, so I dropped her off at her place. I was just about to nose out a coffee shop, when a text pinged in from Marco.

Emergency.

I frowned at the readout. I swore if this emergency had anything to do with donkeys…

Real one, he texted, as if reading my thoughts. *Police are at the salon.*

That did it. I made a hard right, and fifteen minutes later was pulling up in front of Fernando's of Beverly Hills.

As I stepped into the salon, Marco practically ran around the reception desk to meet me at the door, his two-inch neon yellow heels clacking on the floor beneath a pair of black skinny jeans, a white T-shirt with a photo of vintage "Like a Virgin" Madonna on it, and hoop earrings that hung down to his shoulders. "Thank gawd you're here. Mom is at DEFCON three today."

"Oh no." I said. "What happened?"

"What *didn't* happen?" Marco pursed his pink lips. "Nightmare, Mads. Pure nightmare."

"Where's Mom?"

"In the back. Those cops just left."

I let out a little sigh of relief that they hadn't taken her with them in handcuffs.

Marco took my hand. "Come on, doll." He pulled me along behind him. "Mrs. Rosenblatt is trying to calm her down in one of the massage rooms."

We stepped into the third room on the left, and as soon as I saw what was going on, I stopped short. Mostly because, honestly, I had no idea what was going on.

The lights were dimmed, and Mom was lying on the massage table surrounded by small stones and crystals of various colors. Clear crystals made a perimeter around her upper body, an orange one sat on her stomach, and two dark stones were placed at her feet. Mrs. Rosenblatt chanted something and placed a purple amethyst on Mom's forehead. I watched Mom's eyes cross as she followed the path it took.

"Uh…hi?" I said.

Mrs. Rosenblatt looked up. "Maddie, thank goodness you're here. Betty could use some good energy."

"What's going on?" I asked, coming up to Mom and grabbing a hand.

She glanced my way, careful not to turn her head and lose the crystal between her eyes.

"Hi, honey."

"You okay?" I asked.

Mom nodded, the amethyst slipping a little. "Much better now that Mrs. Rosenblatt is cleaning my chakra."

"Those suckers were blocked like a sewage pipe," Mrs. Rosenblatt added.

I tried not to laugh at the very Zen description.

"The detectives were in here again this morning," Mom said. "I get the feeling that they think I'm a suspect!"

"Shhh," Mrs. R admonished. "Don't gum up the chakras again."

Mom nodded, smoothing out her brow with effort. "Right. Calm. Cool. Clean." She let out a long breath.

"What did they say?" I asked, wondering just how mounting the case against Mom was becoming.

"They said my fingerprints were on the murder weapon." She smiled unnaturally as she said it, ending with a deep, guttural "*Oooom.*"

"That's good. Breathe out the frustration," Mrs. R told her.

Mom let out a long breath that smelled like coffee and Danish.

"Anything else?" I asked.

"They wanted to know her alibi again," Marco added. "Then they told her not to leave town."

"As if I would! Only guilty people run," Mom said. Then she paused and added an "*Ooooom.*"

"They said they had a witness," Marco added in a mock whisper.

I whipped my gaze to his. "Witness?"

"Ooooooom!" Mom said, louder this time.

"What witness?" I asked, lowering my voice.

"Someone said they saw your mom arguing with Carrington."

I shook my head. "Everyone saw that."

Marco pursed his lips. "No, after the original argument. Later. Just before Carrington was killed."

"Which is a lie!" Mom said, popping up from her prone position, the amethyst clattering to the floor.

"Betty!" Mrs. R yelled.

"I was nowhere near him. I never saw him again. I was cooling off with a frozen lemonade!" Mom cried.

"Deep breaths—" Mrs. R started.

"I can't breathe! I'm a suspect!" Mom started hyperventilating.

"In. Out. Slow. Oooooooom," Mrs. R instructed.

I bit my lip, not sure if the scene made me want to laugh or cry. While Ramirez had told me on several occasions that eyewitnesses were notoriously unreliable, it was just one more nail trying to pin down Mom's coffin. Of course Mom knew the witness had been mistaken, and I knew it…but I wasn't sure Laurel and Hardy knew it.

"Did they ask anything else?" I asked her. "About the antique store maybe?"

Mom paused in her hyperventilating to turn to me. "They asked if I'd ever been to a shop called Yesterday's Something-or-other."

"Treasures," I supplied automatically.

"Yes, that's the one."

"And you haven't, right?"

Mom shook her head. Then she paused. "I don't think so. But, you know how I love vintage shopping. I can't promise I wasn't there one time."

Oh boy. Not exactly a definite no. "Did they mention anything about fake antiques?"

Mom shook her head.

Mrs. Rosenblatt narrowed her eyes at me. "Why? Do the police think that slimy appraiser was faking something?"

"Maybe," I said. "It's all speculation right now."

"Well, I tell you right now, those cops come back here bothering your mom again, and I'll speculate all of their auras!"

I wasn't sure what kind of threat that was, but the fire in Mrs. R's eyes was real enough.

I gave Mom a hug and left her in Mrs. R's capable, if somewhat left-of-center, hands.

Marco followed me out, fanning himself with one hand. "I swear, I'm not sure how much more of this I can take. This is supposed to be a salon, not a madhouse!"

Po-tay-to, pot-ah-to.

"Yesterday the tear machine," Marco went on, "and today the chakras. I'm losing it, Mads."

"Could be worse. The police could be looking at you as a prime suspect," I told him.

He paused. "I'm sorry, Maddie. It's not that I'm unsympathetic."

"I know," I said. And I did. Marco adored Mom and Faux Dad almost like a second pair of parents.

"So, what are we doing to help?"

"We?" I asked.

Marco blinked his long lashes at me. Natural ones, oddly enough. How a man was allowed to have prettier eyes than I was, I didn't know. "Please, Maddie!" he said. "Take me with you. I can't take the crying anymore. It's scrambling my brain."

I glanced at the time on my phone. "Well, I have the auction for my vintage Chanel in a couple of hours, but I did want to see if I could talk to Allison Cash again first…"

"Done! Let's go."

CHAPTER NINE

————

Yesterday's Treasures was busier than it had been the first time I'd been in, though whether it was due to the influx of antiquers in town for the *Extravaganza* or the notoriety of Carrington's demise, I wasn't sure. Mina was alone at the counter, ringing up a pair of porcelain figures for a couple in matching plaid tops and faded mom/dad jeans. Several other patrons wandered the small aisles, and I spotted Lottie LaMore, the regular collector, standing in front of a wall of paintings. She turned and spied me, waving in recognition.

"The girl with the Chanel, right?" she asked.

I nodded, thinking I didn't mind that description in the least. "Maddie," I said, offering my hand again. "And this is my friend, Marco."

"Ah!" She nodded. "Had to bring him in to see the treasure trove, huh?" she cackled, her smoker's voice rasping until it ended in a cough.

"Something like that," I said, glossing over our real reason for being there.

"Love the hat," Marco told her.

Today Lottie was dressed in a flowing bohemian style caftan in deep oranges and reds. Silver cuffs adorned both wrists, and she'd accessorized with a pair of brown knee-high boots and a brown felt hat.

"Why thank you, young man," she said tipping the brim toward him. Then she paused, giving him a squinty-eyed look. "It is *man*, right?"

Marco did a mock hair flip, his earrings swaying in the light. "It takes a real man to pull off heels like this, honey."

"Hmm." Lottie nodded. "Just checking. One can never be too sure these days, huh?"

"You here to sell another antique?" I asked her, changing the subject quickly.

But Lottie shook her head. "No, I didn't end up selling the Dilama." She paused. "Didn't like the price Allison gave me."

If Allison had lowballed her anything like she had me, I didn't blame her.

"I actually have it in an auction later this afternoon instead. I just stopped by to let Allison know. Professional courtesy and all."

"That wouldn't happen to be Van Steinberg's auction, would it?" I asked.

"Why, yes, actually. You know him?"

"My Chanel heels are going up for auction this afternoon too," I explained.

"Well, I guess I'll see you there then," she said, giving me a wink with her monster lashes. Then she tipped her hat to Marco and made her way toward the counter, where Mina was finally free.

"She's fun," Marco said.

I wasn't sure if he was being sarcastic or actually enjoyed the fellow fashion eccentric-ista. In fact, I could see Marco being her in about thirty years.

"Her husband was an antique collector. She had an old thirty-thousand dollar sculpture in here the other day that looked like a blob of clay."

Marco stifled a laugh. "Not a fan of modern art, Maddie?"

I shrugged. "I don't get it."

"I'm not surprised," he mumbled.

"What's that supposed to mean?"

"Nothing, dahling!" he backpedaled. "Look, the shopgirl's free." He pointed toward Mina, who had apparently had a very brief chat with Lottie and was once again momentarily available.

I quickly made my way toward her before another shopper could waylay her.

"Maddie." Mina smiled my direction as I approached the counter. "Nice to see you again."

"Thanks, you too. This is my friend Marco," I said and patted Marco's shoulder.

"It's a pleasure to meet you, Marco. I'm Mina."

"Charmed, sweetie." He gave her a limp handshake and a mock bow.

Mina laughed, soaking it in. "What brings you in today?" she asked.

I sat my purse on the countertop. "I was hoping to see Allison."

Mina's smile fell. "I'm sorry, but she's still not here."

"Oh. Did she say why?" I asked, wondering again if she was staying away due to grief or guilt.

Mina looked down at the counter. "No. Actually, I didn't hear from her. She didn't call. She's just…not here."

I frowned. "You haven't heard from her at all?"

Mina shook her head and ran her fingers through the length of her glossy hair. "Not since she called in yesterday morning. Honestly? I'm a little worried about her. I think Mr. Carrington's death is really hitting her hard. It's not like her to just not show up."

"Have you tried to call her?" Marco asked.

She nodded. "I tried a little while ago, but there was no answer. I left a voicemail, so hopefully I'll hear from her soon."

"When she does come in, or when you hear from her, could you please have her give me a call? I'd really like to talk to her," I said.

Mina nodded. "I will. I promise. I'm sure she'll call in soon."

I wasn't quite as sure. Especially if she was hiding out because she'd killed her partner. Or worse…had already skipped town.

* * *

I dropped Marco back off in Beverly Hills at Fernando's before heading to Van Steinberg's Auction House. It had been open for preview all morning, in order for potential bidders to examine the items up for sale today and make notes on which antiques they'd like to bid on. Once the auction started, patrons would be able to silently bid on items and, hopefully in my case, fight for them and drive up the prices. Just in case that didn't happen, Van Steinberg and I had agreed on a minimum reserve price, in case the bidding never came near the amount the heels were worth.

After circling the parking lot twice, I finally found a spot near the back, where someone was pulling out. I nudged my minivan in with just enough room to squeeze myself between my driver's side door and the Tesla beside me.

Inside the auction house, a greeter wearing a black suit and tie directed me to the registration desk, where I traded my address, phone number, and driver license number for a white paddle with a number *34* on it in bold black letters. While I was honestly there more to watch, learn, and listen, it was my shopping motto to always be prepared. Who knew? Maybe I'd sell my heels for enough to pick up a small lot of vintage jewelry.

With paddle in hand, I followed the steady stream of people into a larger room to the right that reminded me of a small high school auditorium. A hum of low voices added to the feel, as people discussed their bidding options in low tones. Oil paintings of various landscapes adorned the walls, and blue and chrome chairs lined up in perfect rows on either side of a red carpeted aisle. A tall wooden podium sat at the front of the room, and beside it sat a long table draped in a simple white cloth, just waiting for the treasures of the afternoon to be placed upon it for bid.

"It's a pleasure to see you again." Mr. Van Steinberg stepped up beside me in a perfectly pressed gray suit and steel blue tie. His black shoes were polished, his freshly trimmed goatee twitched ever so slightly with anticipation, and there was a distinct twinkle in his eyes. If everyone here was paying the same commission I was, he was in line to make a nice chunk of change that afternoon. Were I in his place, I was sure I'd have a twinkle in my eyes too.

"Nice to see you too," I told him. I looked around the room. "I'm not an expert, but this looks like a good turnout."

He nodded enthusiastically. "You're right. We had a decent showing last night and a full house this afternoon. Though, I'm not surprised. We have some wonderful pieces going up today. Including your shoes." He smiled.

I hoped someone else thought so too. Preferably someone with deep pockets.

"I don't suppose you've seen Allison Cash here?" I asked.

"Uh, no. No, I haven't," he said, some of the twinkle slipping from his demeanor at the mention of her name. "Why do you ask?"

"She hasn't been at the shop either," I said, watching him closely.

"Hmmm, yes, well…probably grieving, you know…" He trailed off, eyes darting to another group of bidders walking through the doors.

"I was wondering about the painting and the sculpture that Carrington sold here before he died."

"What?" He turned his attention back to me, though I could see his smile slipping the longer we chatted.

"You said Carrington sold two items here at the last auction?"

"Did I? Oh, well, yes. Uh, it was last month."

"Did he have them authenticated?"

Van Steinberg blinked at me. "I-I don't know what you mean. Carrington was an antiques appraiser."

"So there was no third party involved?"

More blinking. "Why would there be?"

Right. Why *would* anyone disagree with Carrington's appraisals? If he said the antiques were real, no one would dispute it. Which would make it temptingly easy to sell fake items at real prices.

"Now, if you'll excuse me…" Van Steinberg didn't wait to be excused before scurrying toward the door. Though whether it was to greet the latest group of auction goers or get away from the discussion about Carrington and Cash, I wasn't sure.

I tried not to take it personally and took the few moments before the auction started to browse the brochure of the day's items. Van Steinberg hadn't just been blowing smoke when he'd said there were some nice items up today. Several paintings, The Blob sculpture I'd seen Lottie with, a handful of older furniture—including some midcentury modern desk from Frank Gehry and a pair of Chippendale armoires—and several pieces of fine jewelry. Apparently Van Steinberg did a fine business here. One that might have suffered had it come out that he was selling fakes at his auction house.

If either of the items Carrington had put up for auction recently were reproductions, and that information had gotten back to Van Steinberg, it was his reputation on the line. No one would frequent auctions where the items were of dubious origin.

Of course, that was assuming Van Steinberg hadn't known about the fakes all along. What if Van Steinberg had known? What if Carrington's *real* business partner was the auction house owner? Who better to be in a position to sell for top dollar? And who better to be able to create an authentic looking fake—an appraiser and auction house owner. No one would argue with them. Unless, of course, someone had figured out their item was a reproduction and Van Steinberg had killed Carrington in an effort to make the dead man take the fall and cover up his own involvement.

Again I wondered who had called in that tip to Laurel and Hardy. It had to have been someone in the know. The owner of the fake itself? Someone close to Carrington? Or close to Van Steinberg?

I looked around at the assembled crowd. Ushers, assistants, the auctioneer. And the bidders. Most looked to be in their late sixties to early eighties, probably retired. A few younger folks spotted the crowd here and there. Some chatted animatedly to each other, likely regulars to the auctions here. I spotted a brown felt hat and waved at Lottie as she caught my eye. She gave me an exaggerated wink, her lashes going slightly crooked in the process.

The large doors to the auction room closed, and a young woman in a plain black pantsuit addressed the crowd, letting us know it was time to take our seats. A couple of beats later, Mr. Van Steinberg stepped up to the podium, and the room went completely silent.

"The first item up for bid is this exquisite modern artwork by…"

As he went on to describe the piece of art beside him, I watched bidders making notes, nodding in appreciation, and finally bidding as Van Steinberg opened the floor. Paddles went up in rapid succession, and Van Steinberg's voice worked overtime to rattle off bids as the price rose higher and higher. Finally a woman with a full head of white hair and a beautiful paisley scarf around her neck won, and she stood and did a little bow to the crowd as they politely clapped. Then we were quickly on to the next item, the Chippendale armoire, where the whole process began again.

I watched as one item after another took the stage, quickly being bid upon and sent off to await their new owners. Several pieces inspired bidding wars, where the prices climbed into territories my bank account would cringe at. Though quite a few items went for under what I'd expect, the interest not as high.

About mid-auction, Lottie's Blob came up to the podium. I saw her lean forward in her seat, clearly excited to see what she'd get for it today. Van Steinberg gave a very long description of its origin and symbolism before beginning the bidding at $1,000. While I thought that was generous, several paddles went up at once, the auctioneer's voice bouncing from one to the other as the prices escalated. After we hit five figures, several paddles went down, but I noticed three bidders duking it out for the ownership. One was the same white haired lady who'd won the first item. The second was a man near the front row in a Hawaiian shirt—clearly enjoying his retirement. I craned my neck to a get a good look at the third as his paddle went up again.

And I nearly fell out of my seat when I did.

It was Bradley Cooper!

Okay, well, maybe not *the* Bradley Cooper, but he was tall, had sandy hair, blue eyes, and an impish smile that looked like it could melt Lady Gaga's heart. My pulse sped up as I wondered if this was the same guy Mom had described as being at the *Antiques Extravaganza*—both on the convention center floor *and* near her in the food court. While it had seemed like a wild goose chase at the time, now it felt like a tangible lead.

A lead who had just won Lottie's antique sculpture for a cool seventy grand. I wasn't sure what shocked me more—my good luck at seeing the actor look-alike or the price for the glazed blob.

As soon as the clay piece was removed from the elegant table and the next item brought in, I watched Bradley Cooper get up and quickly make his way toward a side exit door.

I froze. I did a mental eenie meenie minie moe between staying for the next few items—my Chanel pumps were only three away—or following my one good lead. In the end, the image of Mom's tear-stained face won out, and I made quiet apologies to the other people in my row as I shuffled past them and out the same door I'd seen Bradley Cooper use.

The main lobby was quiet and nearly empty. I whipped my gaze from left to right, hoping for any glimpse of the mystery man. An elderly man exiting the restroom. A woman talking in hushed tones on a cell phone near the reception desk. A portly guy sipping from a coffee cup near the elevator.

And a sandy haired man in a navy suit slipping out the front doors.

I bolted toward them, trying to follow him. Unfortunately, my heels were not made for bolting, and it took several small jogs forward before I hit the glass door, just in time to see Bradley Cooper get into a shiny silver Mercedes.

"Wait!" I called, still hustling in his direction.

But he must not have seen me, as he didn't so much as turn my way, instead roaring the luxury vehicle to life and pulling it out of the lot and onto West Olympic.

And disappearing.

CHAPTER TEN

————

I tried to quell my disappointment as I stood panting on the sidewalk. I took a minute to get my breathing under control, then slunk back into the auditorium, just in time to catch the tail end of bidding for the midcentury modern Gehry desk.

As I silently watched the next item come up, my mind turned over the possibilities of just who Bradley Cooper was. I was dying to ask Van Steinberg, but I'd have to cool my jets until the end of the auction for that. Mom had said she'd seen Bradley Cooper at the *Antiques Extravaganza* show, and now he was here. Possibly a coincidence—Van Steinberg had mentioned that the antiques community was a small one. Or possibly there was more to it. Hadn't Van Steinberg mentioned that, like The Blob that Bradley Cooper had just won, the last piece Carrington had put up for auction was from the Heffernan Studios? Maybe Bradley Cooper hadn't been at the *Extravaganza* to have a piece appraised but to speak to the man he'd just bought a valuable sculpture from...or possibly a fake sculpture?

I was liking that theory more and more, when item number twenty-four came up to the table, and I saw my Chanel shoes. Van Steinberg did them proud, rattling off facts about how they were the signature two-toned look in the late fifties, created with the express purpose of making a woman's legs look longer and her feet look smaller. Bidding started at fifty dollars, and at first I was worried that was all I was going to get. Maybe Allison Cash hadn't lowballed me after all.

But, thanks to a raised paddle by the white haired woman in the scarf, the ball began rolling, and several more paddles slowly went up. I felt the anticipation building in my stomach, understanding the thrill that kept frequent bidders coming back as the price climbed higher and higher. In that moment, it felt like the sky was the limit.

In the end, five hundred dollars was the limit, as Van Steinberg banged his gavel down on the podium, signaling that a lovely woman in a floral sundress had won the item and would be taking my sling-backs home. Any sadness I might have felt at letting them go dissipated as I calculated just how many diapers that five hundred would buy.

A few more items rounded out the auction, and by the time it ended, my backside was beginning to get numb, and my legs were stiff. The crowd slowly began dispersing, making their way as one mass back toward the lobby—some leaving right away, not having bought or sold anything. Others congregated near the reception desk, where paperwork awaited them to claim their newly purchased items.

I caught up to Van Steinberg as he stood by the door, nodding polite goodbyes to the regulars.

"Maddie," he said, beaming at me as I approached. "I'm very pleased with how the bidding went."

"Me too," I told him, meaning it.

"Come by on Sunday, and we'll settle the ticket," he told me.

"Thank you," I said again. "I will. And I was wondering if I could ask you about a bidder?"

Some of the jubilation left his face. "Was there a problem?"

"No, no problem," I assured him. "I just wondered if you knew his name. He actually left early. Sandy hair, about six feet tall."

He frowned. "Sorry, I'm not sure I know who that could be."

"Kind of looks like Bradley Cooper," I tried.

The frown deepened for a brief second before recognition finally set in. "Oh, yes. You must mean Benton."

Bingo. "Benton?" I asked, fishing for more.

Van Stenberg nodded. "Yes. Giles Benton. He's an auction broker."

Something clicked from the last time we'd talked. "You mean he's one of those people who bids for buyers who wish to remain anonymous?"

"Quite right. I'm not surprised he left early. Generally brokers are at an auction for one specific piece, directed by their clients."

"I noticed he won the sculpture from the Heffernan Studios. Did he win the last one as well? The Bracington that Carrington brought in before his death?"

His white eyebrows drew together in a frown. "Actually I believe Benton did have the winning bid for the Bracington sculpture as well. Why do you ask?"

"Just a fan of modern art." I blinked innocently at him, giving him a big smile with teeth and all.

I wasn't sure he totally bought it, but someone else hailed his attention just then, and I quickly excused myself, heading toward my car.

The midday sun had baked the interior to a balmy hundred plus, and I cranked up the AC full blast as I pulled out my phone, typing the name *Giles Benton* into a search engine. It took only a couple of minutes before I found an address for a place in The Valley. Benton may not have been the collector who received fake pieces from Carrington…but he just might work for him.

I typed the address into my GPS and pulled out of the lot.

* * *

Giles Benton's office was located in a modest three story building in Van Nuys, surrounded by decaying apartment buildings and liquor stores. After circling the block a couple times, I finally found a place on the street three doors up and fed the parking meter. Then I backtracked to his building and took the stairs to the offices on the second floor that Google had directed me to. The hallway was carpeted in dark Berber that looked like it had suffered some water damage at some point. The paint on the walls was a dull gray, and the fluorescent lighting buzzed with a threat to go out at any minute.

The door to unit 217 simply read *G. Benton* on the nameplate, and I slowly pushed inside to find a small reception room holding a metal desk, a murky looking fish tank, and a brown sofa that looked like it might have predated the water damage. I stood quietly for a moment, but when no sign of life appeared, I called out a tentative "Hello?"

Rustling came from beyond a door marked *Private Office*, and it opened to reveal my Bradley Cooper look-alike.

Though, up close I could see that all of the boyish charm that had made the real Bradley Cooper famous was missing from this guy's face. In fact, the narrowed blue eyes turned my way felt decidedly suspicious…with a possible undercurrent of danger, as I took in the broad shoulders and bulked biceps beneath his button down shirt that had been hidden under his blazer at the auction house.

"What do you want?" he asked, his voice holding a slight East Coast accent and an edge that had me instinctively taking a step back toward the door.

"Uh, I, uh, got your name from Van Steinberg. He said you're an antiques broker?"

The suspicions didn't recede any. "You in the market to sell something?"

"Buy, actually." I licked my suddenly dry lips. "I was interested in a piece you purchased at auction recently. A Bracington sculpture."

If it was possible, the eyes narrowed further, making me feel as if they could almost see right through me. "I'm sorry. That was for a client."

He turned and started to walk back into this office.

"Wait," I implored him.

He paused, giving me his attention again, though he crossed his arms over his chest and took a wide stance that felt distinctly defensive.

"I'd love to make an offer to your client for the piece," I lied, trying to come up with a plausible story quickly.

"What kind of offer?"

I sucked in a deep breath, hoping for inspiration. I had no idea what the piece was worth or what he'd paid for it at the previous auction. All I had to go on was what he'd just bid for Lottie's Blob. "Sixty thousand," I finally blurted out.

He was silent a beat. I wasn't sure it was a negotiation tactic or if he was just trying to figure out if I was pulling his leg.

"Sixty-five," he shot back. "And my client might consider it."

Considering my bank account held just enough to pay this month's preschool tuition and possibly buy a tube of lip gloss afterwards, a small bubble of anxiety formed in my stomach as I bluffed. "Sixty-five it is." I paused. "But I'd like to talk to the owner in person."

"No deal." Benton turned and started to walk back into his office a second time.

I sighed. "Wait!"

He did, just inside the doorframe, turning to face me as he leaned against it.

"Look, all I want is a name. Just tell me who bought the Bracington, and I'll agree to seventy thousand," I said, upping the ante.

But either he could see right through my charade, or he had impeccable ethics, as he just shook his head. "I don't give out client names. That's the entire reason they come to me. Discretion."

"Not even for seventy grand?" I said.

"No." He pushed off the doorframe and took a step toward me. "And as a collector, you should know and appreciate that."

"Sure, right." I backpedaled, physically and metaphorically, as I took a couple short steps backward toward the door, realizing his stride was long and could reach me in a heartbeat. "Discretion, discretion, discretion." I did a weak laugh.

His jaw tightened, and those eyes narrowed again, suspicion coming off him in waves.

"I, just...I like to know who I'm doing business with," I finished lamely.

"Well, I can tell you who you are *not* doing business with." He took two more steps forward.

I took about six tiny, urgent ones back, feeling my butt come up against the door to the hallway again. "Who?" I managed to get out through the fear suddenly clogging my throat.

He moved toward me again, and I realized I was effectively pinned against the door. He was close enough that I could smell the coffee on his breath and the faint odor of cigarette smoke lingering in his hair.

"Me," he said on a sneer.

And before I had a chance to react, he had the door open, and I was stumbling out into the hallway.

I tripped backward on my heels, just managing to catch my balance before my backside hit the stained carpeting. By the time I'd regained my footing, Benton had slammed the door shut, and, if I wasn't mistaken, I heard the distinct sound of a lock being thrown on the other side.

So much for customer service. I took a deep, shuddering breath, feeling immensely safer in the hallway. I quickly jogged to the stairs, my three-inch pumps echoing in the empty stairwell all the way to the first floor, where I was grateful to push out into the warm sunshine again.

I power walked to my car, not able to shake that anxious feeling until I had the doors locked and the AC on. I breathed deeply, my eyes going to the window on the second floor, which I now knew housed G. Benton's bleak office. I could well see that guy stabbing someone without blinking a blue eye. Though, what motive he had as middleman I wasn't sure. Except, maybe he'd been the middleman for murder as well? What if the disgruntled collector hadn't wanted to get his hands dirty and had hired Benton to off Carrington for him? It was entirely possible Benton had other skills beyond winning auction bids.

If only I knew who his buyer was.

I nibbled on my bottom lip, that thought taunting me as I contemplated my next move. The twins didn't need picked up for another couple of hours. I could check in on Mom, but I trusted Faux Dad to let me know if the police came nosing around again. I was just thinking about a burger and a cold milkshake, when I saw a delivery van pull down the street and double park in front of Benton's office building. While the parking violation was notable, it was the writing on the side of the van that caught my eye.

Van Steinberg's Auction House.

I craned my neck trying to see as a guy in a blue uniform exited the driver's side and went to the back of the vehicle, pulling open the double doors. Then he extracted a large item wrapped in plastic. If I had to guess, it was exactly the size of The Blob Benton had just won. I watched as the delivery guy disappeared inside the building. About five minutes later, he reemerged without the package, hopped back into his van, and left.

I grabbed a piece of gum from my purse, popping it into my mouth as I looked up at Benton's window. While the blinds were half closed, I could make out his shadow crossing the room to a desk near the window and putting his hand up to his ear, as if talking on a phone. If only I were a spy, I could have planted some sort of bug in Benton's office and would be able to hear who he was currently informing about the delivery. Or a cop with a wiretap. Or a lip-reader.

I was just wondering where one would take lip-reading lessons (I think the heat and car exhaust was starting to get to my brain), when Benton lowered his phone to the desk and stepped away from the window.

I waited a couple more minutes to see if he returned, but when I saw him next, it was not as a silhouette on the window shade but as he emerged from the front of the building, the Blob-sized package in his arms. He jogged across the street to his Mercedes parked at the curb, shoved the package into the backseat, and slipped inside. A moment later the car started, and he pulled away from the curb, heading east on Oxnard.

Without thinking, I turned my engine over and pulled into traffic, following him. I felt hope renewed in my chest, mixed with a healthy dose of ohmigod-what-am-I-doing as I tried to stay a couple car lengths behind him and out of his sight. I wasn't sure he'd recognize me through the windshield, but I didn't want to take any chances.

We wound through Sherman Oaks and Studio City, passing through a residential area and onto Ventura. My stomach growled as we made a left and passed a McDonald's, the scent of fresh french fries wafting towards me through my open window.

But I stayed with my prey, following him as he made a right at the next light, heading into the Hollywood Hills.

It was harder to stay out of sight there, the road narrowing. I pulled back, trying to keep enough distance between us that he didn't feel like he was being followed, while still maintaining enough view of him to notice if he turned off on a side street.

Concrete and traffic gave way to oak trees and multimillion-dollar mansions clinging to the side of cliffs to capitalize on the view of downtown from expansive decks and infinity pools. The air was warm and held a faint scent of cedar drying in the sunshine. I struggled to keep an eye on the luxury car as winding roads full of hairpin turns obscured my view. It was only luck that Benton turned off the main road onto a straightaway, allowing me to keep him in sight. If he'd done it a moment earlier, I'd never have seen and sailed right on by.

As he led me down a smaller street, I realized I recognized the area. I'd been down this road a few times in the past, and as Benton pulled to a stop in the circular drive of a home that sat as a glass and chrome monument to modern architecture overlooking the entire valley, I realized I'd even been to this particular house before.

My first visit had been several years ago while investigating a death on the set of Ricky's TV show. My most recent visit to this home had ended in a bittersweet goodbye just before I'd married Ramirez.

I took a deep breath, pushing nostalgia to the side as I pulled over next to a tall oak tree and watched Benton remove the package from his car, taking it to the front door. He rang the bell, only having to wait a moment before it was opened by the home's owner.

Felix Dunn.

CHAPTER ELEVEN

———

I watched Benton and Felix exchange a few words that I couldn't hear, Benton do some gesturing to the package, and Felix shake his hand. Then Felix took the wrapped item inside the house and closed the door. Benton hopped back into his Mercedes and sped off down the road the way we'd come.

It was all over so fast, yet I was still stuck staring at the house, trying to rearrange all of my theories. Felix Dunn was Benton's anonymous buyer. Clearly Felix had not killed Carrington. Not that he didn't have a bit of a wicked streak when it came to printing salacious stories in his tabloid, but he certainly wasn't a cold-blooded killer.

Though, honestly, I never would have pegged him as an antiques collector either.

Left with more questions than answers, I got out of my car and walked up the paved drive to Felix's home, ringing the bell, as I'd seen Benton do just moments before. I heard the sound of footsteps echoing on the other side before the door opened and Felix stared down at me.

"Maddie?" He blinked at me, a small frown of confusion forming between his sandy eyebrows. His hair was styled differently than the last time I'd seen him, falling just a little long into his eyes. It suited him—made him seem younger than the laugh lines at the corners of his eyes said he was. Though, he was dressed just as I'd remembered—in his usual uniform of rumpled looking khaki pants, a loose dress shirt, untucked and in need of a good ironing, and sneakers that looked more appropriate for a skateboarding teen than the editor in chief of LA's most popular tabloid.

"Hi," I said, giving him a big smile. "How are you?"

"Uh, fine, I guess. W-what are you doing here?" He looked behind me, as if the answer might lie in his empty driveway.

"It's a long story," I told him honestly. "May I come in?"

"Uh, yes. Yes, of course." He stepped back to allow me entry, his British accent coming out a bit thicker than normal, having been caught unawares.

"Listen, I don't mean to bother you—" I started.

"No bother," he cut in, ever the one with the well-bred manners. He paused, giving me a head-to-toe glance. "You look good."

I cleared my throat, the compliment meaning more to me than it should. "Thanks."

"Can I offer you a drink or something…" He trailed off, and I could see him mentally going over what his "or something" options might be. As a bachelor, I doubted his refrigerator held much more than condiments.

I shook my head, giving him an out. "No, thank you. Actually, this isn't exactly a social visit."

"Oh?" One eyebrow rose, disappearing into his too long bangs. "Everything alright?"

"Well, yes. And no."

"Does this have to do with your mother?"

I nodded and quickly filled him in on what I'd learned since asking for Cam's photos the day before. Which, honestly wasn't much, but when I got to following Benton from his office and my theory about an angry antiques collector, that frown was back on his face again.

"So, you thought I killed Carrington?" he asked.

"Not *you*," I said. "But, yeah, I thought it was a good lead that a collector might not have been happy about getting fakes."

"And you're thinking Benton had something to do with it?"

I sucked in a deep breath. "Maybe. How well do you know him?"

Felix ran a hand through his hair. "Well, we're not school chums, if that's what you mean. I met him through a mutual acquaintance. He's a good broker. Gets things at a fair price. And charges a very low commission."

I stifled a laugh. Felix was notorious for being stingy when it came to money. Ironic, considering he had plenty of it. In fact, as I'd found out years before, he owned an actual castle in England and was even distantly related to the queen.

"So, you liked Benton's low commissions and hired him to pick up antiques for you. Including a Bracington sculpture."

"Yes. I acquired that just last month." He paused. "How did you know?"

"It was Carrington's. He put it in Van Steinberg's auction. How many other pieces did Benton acquire for you?"

Felix shrugged. "Just a couple. With the stock market as volatile as it is, I thought I'd diversify my investments."

"Were the items from Carrington?"

"Haven't the foggiest. Until you said it now, I had no idea the Bracington had been."

I pursed my lips together, unsure how he'd react to my next question. "How confident are you that the Bracington is real?"

He stared at me for a beat before answering, "One hundred percent."

"That's a big percent," I pointed out.

"Yes, well, I told you, they are investments. I don't take money matters lightly. I've had everything that I've purchased independently appraised since acquiring."

"Even the Bracington sculpture?" I asked, feeling my one and only lead slipping from my grasp.

Felix nodded. "Yes. Just last week in fact. Turns out I even paid a bit below market value." He beamed, as if he'd gotten an A on a report card.

"And it's definitely legit?"

He nodded again, his hair flopping in his eyes. "Like I said, one hundred percent."

I sighed, feeling my entire body sag. So much for that theory.

"Would you like to see it?" Felix asked.

I wasn't sure what I'd see that an appraiser wouldn't, but I agreed anyway, following him from the open living room to a smaller room off the chef's kitchen that no one cooked in.

"How much do you trust Benton?" I asked, still hanging on to a shred of hope that the menacing broker had something to do with Carrington's death.

"Like I said, I don't know him that well. But I trust his instincts when it comes to antiques."

"He was at the *Antiques Extravaganza*," I pointed out. "Mom saw him more than once."

"It's possible he was scouting items," Felix reasoned.

Which I hated to admit, was actually very reasonable.

Felix stepped into a smaller room and flicked on the lights, revealing a study. A large polished desk in one corner, lots of expensive looking leather bound books on the shelves, and a bright picture window that looked out onto his pool. He walked to the far wall, stopping in front of a glazed clay sculpture that sat on a pedestal. While it was taller and skinnier than The Blob, it had the same indistinct shape about it, and I was still confident that Max and Livvie could pump out something equally symbolic with Play-Doh.

"It's…nice," I said, trying not to be rude.

"Isn't it?" Felix beamed like a proud papa as he stared at it. "It's been incredibly well maintained. See this part here? How thin it is?" he asked, pointing to about mid-statue. "A lot of pieces from the Heffernan Studios have broken over time. They're very delicate. But that's what makes it so valuable."

I nodded. I'd heard that before when watching the *Antiques Extravaganza* on TV. Age played a much smaller factor in value than condition and rarity. "I hate to say it, but I just don't get modern art," I admitted.

"That's okay." Felix turned to me with a smile. "I don't get fashion." He gave me a wink.

I couldn't help laughing at the easy banter. "Okay, so you're sure there's no way this could be fake?" I checked again.

But Felix shook his head. "No. It was authenticated by the Bracington estate themselves."

Which meant I was back to square one.

I thanked Felix for his time and promised not to be such a stranger as he walked me out. A promise that we both knew was probably hollow, as our particular memory lane felt a little too dangerous to traverse very often.

I walked back to my car, turned on the AC, and headed back down the hill, my mind adjusting to what I'd seen in Felix's house.

Carrington had definitely not sold fake antiques to Benton. At least not in this case.

That is, if, in fact, there ever were any fakes to begin with. While it made for a great motive for murder, all I really had was some vague tip phoned in to Laurel and Hardy. Let's face it, while I had a lot of good theories, all the evidence still pointed in Mom's direction. What I needed to know was what, if anything, had really been faked.

And for that, I needed to talk to Allison Cash.

* * *

Half an hour later I was parked in front of a small Spanish style house with a red tile roof, dark shutters, and a lot of overgrown birds of paradise looming over a short wooden fence. No car sat in the driveway, and the windows were all dark. I checked the address Google had given me for Allison a second time, making sure I had the right place. 614 Aldercroft Drive. I wasn't sure where I'd imagined the severe looking woman living, but this felt a lot more homey and less disciplined than I imagined.

I got out and locked my car with a beep, opening the wooden gate and following a stone pathway studded with weeds to the front door. I knocked and waited, listening.

No sound of footsteps, no rustling of someone getting up, no faint sounds of a TV in another room. I tried the bell, but the echoing chime through the wooden door was all I heard.

I stepped over a potted plant and two newspapers on the porch, putting my hands to my eyes as I peeked in the window at the right of the door. I could make out a sofa, a television, a coffee table. Beyond the living room, a small dining set was visible, though no dishes or placemats sat on it. Everything looked clean, quiet, and empty.

"She's not home."

I quickly pulled back from the window, feeling guilty at being caught looking in. A woman stood in the yard next door, a pair of pruning shears in one hand. Her floppy straw hat flapped in the warm breeze, and the knees of her jeans bore the grass stains of a dedicated gardener.

"Sorry. I was just looking for Allison Cash," I said.

"She's not here," the woman repeated.

"Do you happen to know where she went?"

The woman shook her head, taking off a pair of gardening gloves.

"Any clue when she'll be back?"

"I have no idea," she told me. "She usually asks me to bring in her mail and her newspapers when she goes out of town, but she didn't ask this time."

"Did you see her leave?" I pressed.

She just shook her head. "No. But I haven't seen her come home from work the last couple of days, and her newspapers are piling up." She gestured to the two I'd just stepped over.

She was right—it didn't look like anyone had been home in at least a couple of days. And Allison hadn't been to work either.

So where was Allison Cash?

CHAPTER TWELVE

———

I thanked the neighbor and handed her my card, asking her to call if she saw Allison come home. Then I drove to the Starbucks down the street for a much-needed afternoon caffeine infusion before picking up the kids. I'd just paid for my iced coffee and was heading back to my car when my phone rang, and Ricky's number came up.

I frowned, hoping everything was okay with Dana. "Hey, Ricky," I answered.

"Hi, Maddie! How are you?"

"Melting," I answered, beeping my car open and slipping inside the roasting interior.

Ricky laughed. "Join the club. I heard it was 105 in Palmdale today."

"Well, I guess life could be worse. We could be in Palmdale."

"Seriously."

"So, what's up?" I asked, sipping my drink.

"Dana's not answering her phone. I was wondering if you could put her on?"

"Me?" I asked.

"She is with you, right?"

"No, last I saw her, she and Marco were arguing about—" I froze, stopping myself just in time. "Uh…arguing about shoes?" I finished lamely, trying to mentally pull my foot out of my mouth.

"Arguing about shoes," Ricky repeated, not totally buying it.

"Uh, yep. At the shoe store. Where we were at. Together. Today. Earlier. But, you know, not now. But we were."

"Maddie, you're a terrible liar."

Oh crap, crap, crap. "W-what do you mean?" I asked, channeling dumb blonde as hard as I could.

"It was about the party, wasn't it?"

I cleared my throat. "Party? What party?"

"My surprise birthday party."

I closed my eyes and thought a dirty word, trying not to picture my best friend's face as she realized the cat had clawed its way out of the bag. "How did you find out?" I moaned.

"Well, the way Dana's been sneaking out early, making hushed phone calls, and snapping her laptop shut every time I walked into a room, I figured she was either having an affair or planning a surprise party."

"There's no affair," I assured him.

"I know." He paused. "I saw the receipt for the cake on her kitchen counter last week."

"You cannot tell Dana you know," I pleaded with him. "She's been planning this for weeks."

I heard shuffling on the other end, like the phone being shifted to the other ear. "Hey, I'm not about to spoil anyone's fun."

"Good," I told him. "I expect to see an Oscar-worthy performance of shock and awe when you walk in."

"Geez, you're more demanding than my agent," he joked. Then he asked, "So, what exactly were she and Marco arguing about?"

I bit my lip. "You don't want to know."

"That bad?"

"Let's just let some things stay a surprise."

*   *   *

I picked up the twins from preschool, and while they went to town on a couple of coloring books, I spent the rest of the afternoon working on some sketches for my upcoming line of high heeled winter boots. But my heart wasn't really in it. My mind kept going to the missing Allison Cash, the dead Peter Carrington, and my mom caught in the middle of it all.

By the time Ramirez walked in the door with—God bless the man—a large pizza in hand, I'd made very little headway on either my suede ankle boot or the question of Carrington's death.

"Is that pepperoni?" I asked as he stooped to plant a kiss on my cheek before depositing the pizza on the counter.

"Uh-huh. With sausage and mushroom."

Be still my beating heart. I abandoned my sketchbook and followed him to the kitchen, where he'd already grabbed two plates and a pile of napkins. He extracted one gooey slice and set it on a plate before passing it to me.

"This isn't to butter me up for anything in particular, is it?" I asked, digging into the cheese covered heaven.

He shook his head. "I wish. It's mostly to soften the blow."

I paused mid-chew. "Oh no. What now?"

Ramirez served himself a slice. "Word at the station is Laurel and Hardy have a witness in Carrington's murder."

I swallowed my bite of pizza that suddenly felt like cardboard. "Mom mentioned something about that earlier. She said someone claims to have seen her with Carrington."

He nodded.

"But they're lying," I said, pointing my slice of pizza at him for emphasis.

"Or mistaken about who they saw. Or what they saw or when they saw it," Ramirez added. "You know witnesses. Memories aren't always reliable."

"But it isn't helping Mom's case any, is it?" I asked.

Ramirez shook his head slowly. "Sorry, babe."

I took another bite of pizza, needing comfort food.

"And there's more."

I glared at Ramirez over the top of my slice. "More?" I asked, my mouth full.

"Laurel and Hardy are naming an official suspect in Carrington's death."

"Tell me it's Allison Cash?"

He shook his head slowly again. "Wish I could, kid. But they like your mom for this."

"My mom did not kill anybody," I said vehemently.

Ramirez held his hands up in a surrender gesture. "I know, I know. But it's out of my hands. Trust me, I've been trying to run interference as much as a guy who is off the case can."

While I knew Ramirez was doing everything humanly possible to keep my mom out of jail, I just wasn't sure it would be enough.

"What does 'official suspect' mean?" I asked.

Ramirez pursed his lips together like he'd rather not say.

I set my slice of pizza down on my plate. "Come on. I'm a big girl. I can take it." Maybe.

"They'll be going public with her name."

I sucked in a breath, thinking the kind of words I didn't dare say out loud around my preschoolers. "I'll call Faux Dad and see if he can keep her off social media."

"Good luck," Ramirez told me. "You know she's addicted to those Facebook polls. She posts, like, three a day."

I did know. I also knew she'd be devastated if she saw her own face come up in her news feed next to the word *murderer*. It was one thing to have a couple of buffoons in blue think you were guilty. It was another to have the world giving you the side eye.

I was about to ask more, when Ramirez's phone rang, and he glanced briefly at the readout before a frown creased his features. "I gotta take this," he mumbled and stepped into the relative quiet of the hallway to swipe the call on.

I took the moment to pull out my own phone, texting Faux Dad the latest. He shot a reply right back, saying he'd do his best to shield her. Which was small comfort as I knew she was bound to see something. And bound to take it to heart. I tried to choke down a couple more bites of pizza, but all the joy had been sucked out of the calories.

A beat later Ramirez came back into the kitchen. As he ended the call, his face was stoic and eyes dark in a way that made my stomach sink.

"What now?" I asked, not totally sure I wanted to know.

"They found Allison Cash."

I did an internal sigh of relief. "Thank God. So, what's she saying about where she's been the past two days?"

"Nothing." Ramirez paused. "Allison Cash is dead."

CHAPTER THIRTEEN

———

The lone slice of pizza I'd had time to ingest sat in my stomach like a lead weight as Ramirez drove through the early evening traffic, and I felt a mix of guilt and confusion solidifying around it. Guilt that I'd known Allison was missing earlier that day and not thought to report it to anyone. Confusion because the reason I hadn't reported it is I'd thought she'd done a runner…not been killed.

If Allison was a victim, that clearly meant someone else had been doing the killing. Had the same person killed Carrington? It would seem like a heck of coincidence if not. Which meant, whatever the motive for Carrington's death, it hadn't been a rift between partners like I'd originally thought. Had the two been up to something together…and a third party found out? I thought of Van Steinberg. If Carrington and Cash had been selling fakes together through his auctions, he had a good reason to want them both out of the picture. If there had been fakes. And if they'd sold anything. And if Van Steinberg had found out.

I glanced over at Ramirez, hesitating to voice any of my theories. I was pretty sure he'd been two seconds away from taking off without me, but I'd been just a beat quicker, simultaneously calling the teenager next door to come watch the twins as I'd slid into the passenger seat of Ramirez's SUV, promising to be a silent observer. He'd paused—both of us knowing full well that was probably not going to happen. But in the end, he'd agreed. Probably because he wasn't fond of sleeping on the couch. Smart man.

The windshield illuminated with red and blue flashing lights as we pulled onto Allison Cash's block. Though, the commotion was not centered around her house but farther down the street, at the entrance to a small neighborhood park. Ramirez pulled up behind a squad car—one of at least a dozen I saw parked up and down the street, mixed in with other official looking vehicles and a news van from channel six.

"Great," Ramirez mumbled under his breath when he saw the van. Then he turned to me. "You're staying here, right?"

"Sure," I responded.

Only as he stepped from the car, so did I.

He shot me a look and sighed. "You're not staying here, are you?"

I shrugged in apology. "If the tables were turned, would you sit in the car with your mom's life on the line?"

It was a bit of a low blow, as I knew Ramirez's biggest soft spot was the seventy-five-year-old white-haired woman living in Hacienda Heights. But it had the desired effect.

Ramirez did another sigh and shook his head. "Fine. But hang back and don't say anything, okay?"

I gave a vigorous nod of consent and a zipping the mouth closed and throwing away the key thing, then followed a step behind him as he approached a group of uniformed officers standing sentry at the entrance to the park.

I listened silently as he identified himself to the small group and asked for a brief rundown of the scene. They used a lot of code and police jargon that went over my head, but I did catch a few key phrases. Like "the deceased," "gunshot wound," and "lividity." I watched them gesture farther into the park, toward a grouping of trees along a fence, where ivy and other vegetation made for what looked like excellent cover for someone wanting to hide a body. Several more uniformed officers stood near the trees, and a couple of plainclothes detectives crouched close to the ground, examining something that I was pretty sure I didn't want to get a closer look at.

I hugged my arms around myself, thinking that when I'd visited Allison's home this afternoon, she'd likely been just a few paces away. And had likely been dead for some time. It had been at least two days since anyone had seen her at home or the antique shop. Had she been here the whole time?

The uniformed officer finished his report, and Ramirez stepped away from him, eyes going to the grouping of trees.

"Do they know how long she'd been here?" I asked, feeling that guilt hit me again.

Ramirez shook his head. "A neighbor walking her dog found the body this evening. ME says it looks like she's been moved. Possibly killed elsewhere and dumped here."

I bit my lip. "She lives just down the street."

He shot me a look. "Do I want to know how you know that?"

"Probably not."

He inhaled deeply, his nostrils flaring with the effort. "Well, it's a good possibility for a primary crime scene. There are drag marks on her back and carpet fibers under her fingernails."

"Carpet? Like, she was killed on a rug?"

"More likely they're from the trunk of a car."

I let that sink in. "Like one she was transported from her house to here in."

He nodded. "There's a road along the back of the park that backs up to the fence over there."

I bit my lip, glancing in the direction he pointed. If the road backed right up to the drop point, it wouldn't have taken someone very strong to pull the body out of the trunk. I'd seen Allison Cash in person. She'd been slim and petite. Even as dead weight, it wouldn't be difficult for just about anyone to lift her in and out of a trunk.

"Any idea when she was moved?" I asked, hoping to cover Mom with an alibi this time.

But he shook his head. "Not yet. ME might get more when he does an autopsy, but at the moment, best he can pin down is that she's been exposed to the elements for at least 24 to 48 hours."

Which was a pretty big window. "Do they still think Mom could be involved?" I asked, dreading the answer.

"*I* don't," he clarified. "But *they* might." He gestured to the group of officers near the trees.

I followed his gaze, spying the two plainclothes detectives straightening up now. One in a rumpled, ill-fitting suit and the other in a severe bun and sensible shoes. Laurel and Hardy. I thought a really dirty word.

"I agree," Ramirez mumbled.

Okay, so maybe I more thought it out loud.

Laurel noticed us and nodded, gesturing to Hardy. Then the two of them made their way across the expanse of lawn toward us.

"Ramirez," Hardy said, addressing my husband as they approached.

"Hardy." Ramirez nodded toward the man's partner. "Laurel."

"What are you doing here?" she asked.

"I got a call about a body."

"*Our* body," Hardy said, puffing his chest out. Which still wasn't far enough to match the girth of his belly.

Ramirez raised one eyebrow ever so slightly in his direction. "*Yours*?"

"That's right," Laurel agreed. "Carrington case."

"I didn't hear any mention of the case," Ramirez stated simply.

I bit my tongue, waiting to see how this played out. I noticed none of the detectives had acknowledged my presence, but at the moment I was kinda fine with that.

"The deceased was Carrington's partner," Hardy informed us, looking very proud of himself for making that connection.

"Alice," Laurel supplied.

"Allison," I corrected automatically.

She frowned, noticing me for the first time, and pulled out her phone, checking her notes.

"Her name doesn't matter," Hardy decided, skimming over the details. "What matters is she and Carrington worked together."

"So you think the perpetrator in both crimes is the same person?" Ramirez asked.

"Of course," Laurel snapped, still frowning at her phone.

"Any evidence of that?"

Both detectives blinked at my husband as if the word were foreign to them.

"How was Ms. Cash killed?" Ramirez asked.

"What?" Laurel asked, looking at her phone again, as if it might hold some answers.

"Cause of death?" Ramirez clarified. "Carrington was stabbed. I assume Allison Cash was as well?"

I tried to stifle a smile, since I knew he'd just been informed that she hadn't been.

"Uh, well, no," Hardy admitted, his gaze going to his partner. "She was shot."

"Really? That is different," Ramirez noted.

"Crime of opportunity," Laurel shot back. "Killer used what was on hand."

"And the killer just happened to have a gun on hand this time and not at the convention center?"

"Now what would a lady like Mrs. Springer be doing carrying a gun around?" Hardy reasoned.

Ramirez nodded. "Good point."

Hardy smiled wide at the seeming praise.

Until Ramirez added, "Mrs. Springer wouldn't be carrying a gun around. Anywhere."

"Now, wait. That's not what I meant," Hardy protested.

"Look, Ramirez," Laurel stepped in. "I know you've got a personal tie to the suspect. But even you can't ignore the evidence."

"Officer Nolan said the bullets appeared to be .44 caliber?" Ramirez asked.

Hardy nodded. "Yeah. But those aren't like any casings I've seen. Weird looking."

"Weird? How so?" Ramirez asked.

"Larger. More powder burns," Laurel piped up.

"So what sort of weapon do you think it came from?"

Hardy shrugged. "Beats me. That's for forensics to figure out."

His ownership of the case was inspiring.

"So, I take it you didn't find a murder weapon at the scene?"

"We haven't found it yet," Laurel said. Then she shot me a pointed look. "But we will."

Despite the buffoonery at work, a chill ran down my back as I thought of Mom. Obviously she didn't own the murder weapon—or any gun for that matter. But I didn't trust Laurel and Hardy to actually worry about minor details, such as innocence.

Let's face it—guilty or not, Mom was in trouble. And it was up to me to get her out.

And quickly.

*   *   *

Ramirez was up and out of the house early the next morning, rising with the sun and leaving with a quick peck on my cheek and a promise that coffee was brewing in the kitchen. Once I heard his car pull out of the driveway, I willed sleep to visit me again, but it was useless. Thoughts of Peter Carrington's smug smirk, Allison Cash's discarded body, and Mom's messy chakra all haunted me, urging me up and out of bed. I dragged myself into a hot shower and applied extra eye makeup to cover up the fact I'd only slept a few fitful hours. I was just throwing on a pair of capri cut skinny jeans and a flowy white tunic top, when I heard the double trouble waking up in the nursery next door.

Two bowls of oatmeal, a dozen apple slices, and an episode of *Paw Patrol* later, I was enjoying my second cup of coffee, when Dana knocked at my front door.

"Ohmigod, I read all about Allison Cash on Twitter. They're saying your mom is an official suspect! What happened?" she demanded all in a rush as she pushed inside.

I quickly filled her in on everything that had happened since I'd seen her last, over a third cup of coffee and another episode of *Paw Patrol*, trying to recall all the details I'd learned last night.

"So they have no idea when Allison was killed?" she asked when I'd finished.

I shook my head. "Not so far. But no one has seen her in two days."

Dana pursed her lips together. "I wonder."

"Hmm?" I asked, sipping my coffee.

"Well, we could have been some of the last people to see her alive."

I thought back to our visit to the shop. "I doubt it. Mina was with her when we left. She didn't mention anything about Allison going home early that day."

"Okay, so she was killed that evening? At home?"

I shrugged. "It would make sense, considering they dumped her body in the park down the street."

"You think a customer that Carrington sold fake items to killed her?" Dana asked.

I shrugged. "Or maybe Benton," I decided, remembering the menace that had come off him in virtual waves. "Maybe Carrington and Cash had some scheme going with him, and it all went south."

"But you said Felix thought the antique he bought was real."

I sighed. "Okay, well, maybe that one was, but something else wasn't?"

"Or maybe there are no fakes at all," Dana reasoned. "We haven't encountered any so far."

"I hate it when you're right." I sipped my coffee, feeling deflated.

"You know," Dana said. "What if we've been going about this all the wrong way?"

"How so?" I sipped my coffee.

"Well, what if Carrington's death had nothing to do with fake antiques at all. What if it was personal?"

I raised an eyebrow her way. "You mean someone just hated both Carrington and Cash enough to kill them?"

"Or loved one of them enough and hated the other," she said.

"Like the Clown Lady."

She nodded. "Right. What if Terri *did* talk to Carrington at the antiques show and he rejected her—called her out as delusional."

"Or insulted one of her clowns," I cut in.

"She kills him in a fit of passion, then later goes after the woman she believed poisoned Carrington against her—Allison."

"I could see it," I agreed.

"There's only one way to find out for sure," Dana said.

I felt a sinking in the pit of my stomach. "Are you sure there aren't two ways? Like, one that doesn't involve going back to the den of clowns?"

CHAPTER FOURTEEN

———

Half an hour later, I'd dropped the kids off at Mom's house—who was only too happy to spend the morning with them and not thinking about dead antique dealers and the ensuing media circus—and Dana and I were facing Terri Voy's myopic gaze again as we stood on her front porch.

"Can I help you?" she asked, her eyes magnified to twice their size behind her large lenses. They were red, and I could tell she'd been crying more since we'd last been there.

"Maddie Springer," I said, jogging her memory. "And this is my friend Dana."

Dana waved beside me.

Terri frowned. "I remember you two." She put her right hand on her hip. "What do you want?"

"I was hoping I could chat with you a bit more?"

"Why?"

While she'd welcomed us with open arms the last time we'd been there, I could see her stance shifting to more defensive now. Though, whether it was guilt or just annoyance at two strangers on her doorstep asking nosey questions, I wasn't sure.

"Are you aware that Allison Cash was found dead last night?" Dana asked.

"Yeah. I saw it on the news." If she had any emotion about the subject, it was well masked.

"We were hoping you could clear up a couple of matters about her."

Terri's eyes narrowed behind her glasses, going from Dana to me. Finally she shrugged and stepped back, allowing us entry. "Fine. But I'm busy, so make it quick."

Trust me. I was not going to linger in the house of a million eyes.

We followed Terri into the living room, where she moved a couple of clown dolls off the sofa to allow us seating. "So what do you want to know?" she asked.

"You didn't have many good things to say about Allison the last time we were here," I noted.

Terri shrugged. "She wasn't a very good person."

"Now she's a very dead person," Dana pointed out.

"Am I supposed to be sad about that?" she asked, eyes narrowing again behind her lenses.

"You clearly hated Allison. Now Allison is dead," Dana said.

"And you think I had something to do with that?" Terri laughed, the sound high pitched and unsettling. Like mania was lurking just on the other side of it.

"Did you?" Dana pushed.

"No," she said emphatically

Which didn't hold a lot of weight, as it was exactly what she'd say if she had killed her.

"Where were you two nights ago?" I asked.

"Is that when she was killed?" Terri asked, shifting her gaze to me.

I nodded. "Last anyone saw of her was that afternoon. At the antique shop."

"Thursday night…" Terri frowned, as if thinking back. "I was here. At home."

"Alone?"

"No. I had my friends with me."

"Can you give us the names of those friends?" Dana said, pulling out her phone to take notes.

Terri frowned in concentration again. "Bubbles, Boo-Boo, Honeypots, Mr. Tickles…"

I blinked at her. Good lord, I think she meant the clown dolls. I looked to Dana. She was staring at Terri, stylus hovering over the phone, the same thought apparently occurring to her.

"Wait—do you mean the dolls?" I asked.

"They are *not* dolls. They're collectibles."

Sure. But they weren't alibis.

"Were any non-collectible friends here with you that night?" I asked. "Like...living ones?"

Terri shrugged. "I didn't have any visitors, if that's what you mean."

"So you were home. Alone. No one saw you?"

Her gaze ping-ponged from Dana to me. "Look, I didn't hurt Allison. I mean, why would I? Peter is already gone." She ended the statement with a sniffle and covered her mouth with her hands.

"Maybe you blamed her for Peter being gone?" I asked.

Her head popped back up at that one. "Well, shouldn't I?" she asked. "She was the one poisoning him. But I didn't kill her. I knew it was only a matter of time before she was going to get what she deserved, the lying, cheating faker."

Something about the way she said *fake* suddenly clicked in the back of my mind.

"What do you mean 'get what she deserved'?" I asked her.

Terri blinked some more at me. "I-I mean karma comes back to you."

"Especially when someone tips off the police that you're a faker," I said, taking a wild stab.

"P-police?" Her voice suddenly sounded small, her gaze going to her clown doll, as if he'd protect her.

"The tip to the police about Yesterday's Treasures selling fake antiques. It was you. You called it in," I said, feeling more confident in the statement now.

"I don't know what you're talking about."

"You wanted to hurt Allison, so you called in the tip."

She stared at me for a long minute, and I thought she was going to tell me to get out of her clown infested house. But finally her shoulders slumped, and she gave in. "Yes. I called in the tip," she confessed. "But it was all true," she rushed to add. "Allison and Peter were really selling fake antiques."

"Why do you say that?" Dana jumped in.

Terri sighed and grabbed the stuffed clown from beside her on the sofa, running her fingers over its curly red hair. "I stopped in to the shop to see Peter one day a couple of months ago. I missed him, you know? I just wanted to see him for a few minutes."

I nodded. "Go on."

"He was appraising a bracelet for a woman. She wanted to sell it to him, but he told her it was a fake. A cheap reproduction. Not worth more than the price of the silver."

I could picture the scene, as he'd said much the same thing to my mom at the show.

"Anyway, a couple weeks later I was at the auction house. I was hoping to get Peter alone for a few minutes." She blushed.

"Did he say something about the bracelet?" Dana asked.

Terri shook her head. "No, I never got to talk to him. He was too busy. But I did see the same bracelet go up in the auction that day."

"Wait—Carrington put the bracelet that he knew was fake up for auction at Van Steinberg's?" I asked.

Terri nodded. "And it sold for a couple thousand dollars."

"Did you tell anyone?" I asked.

Terri bit her lip and slowly shook her head. "Not then. Look, I didn't want to get Peter in trouble. I mean, he was a good person. But after he died…well, I thought it might be important. You know, to find out who killed him. So I called the police."

"Why did you call anonymously?" Dana asked. "Why not give your name?"

Terri looked down at the ground. "I-I wanted to make sure they looked into it. Believe it or not, sometimes I have a hard time getting people to take me seriously."

Shocker.

"Do you remember who won the bid for the bracelet?" I asked.

"Sorry. I didn't get a name." She shook her head again. "But I remember thinking the guy looked familiar. Like he reminded me of some actor."

"Bradley Cooper?" I asked, having a pretty good idea whom she was referring to. "He was in *A Star Is Born.*"

"Yeah, that's the one!" She paused. "I felt bad for him to pay that much for a fake. I never thought Peter would let himself be lured into something that dirty."

"You think someone lured him into it?" Dana asked.

"Well of course. Peter would never do this on his own. It was her!" Terri's voice rose into shrill territory. "She must have put him up to it. I told you, she was poisoning his mind!"

"And now she's dead," I said.

Terri sucked in a breath. "I didn't kill her." She hugged her clown close to her chest. "Now, if you're through, Bobo and I would like very much if you would leave."

* * *

"Well, that was unnerving," Dana said once we were back in my car, AC blasting.

"But interesting," I countered. "At least we know who called Laurel and Hardy now."

"You believe her story about Carrington and the fake bracelet?"

I thought about it for a beat. "I do. Considering how enamored with Carrington she was, I don't see her making up something that makes him look bad."

"True. But I still think it's entirely possible she killed Carrington in a fit of passion, floated the fake antique story to the police as a red herring, and then went after Allison."

I shrugged. "Her alibi for the night of Allison's murder is definitely shaky."

Dana shot me a look. "Ya' think?"

I grinned. "But I'm still inclined to believe her about the fake bracelet. I mean, it would be easy enough to check auction records and verify the bracelet was sold."

"Okay, so let's assume the fakes are real." Dana paused. "So to speak."

"Which means there is a collector out there who was duped by Carrington. At least once."

"You think Van Steinberg has a record of the buyer who won the bracelet?"

I shook my head. "No, if Benton was the broker who purchased it, the buyer would be anonymous in Van Steinberg's records. Benton's the only one who knows the buyer's name. And he was decidedly *not* chatty last time I saw him," I added. I paused, my mind going back to the menacing way he'd ushered me out of his office. "You know, maybe it's more than a coincidence that Benton was the one who brokered the deal for Carrington's fake bracelet."

"How so?"

"Well, what if he and Carrington were in on it together?"

"I like it. Go on."

"Carrington gives Benton a heads-up about a fake antique. Benton finds a buyer. Then they go through the motions at the auction house, using Van Steinberg to help give the item a legit provenance. In the end, they split the proceeds."

"So something goes wrong with a deal, and Benton kills Carrington?" Dana asked.

"Maybe. Or one of Benton's clients finds out and kills Carrington."

"So where does Allison fit in?" Dana asked.

I shrugged. "Maybe she was in on it too? Or maybe she saw something while she was at the *Extravaganza*? Saw Benton go after Carrington, so he had to kill her too?"

"You know, if the bracelet is really only worth a couple thousand dollars, I find it hard to believe someone would kill over that," Dana said, pulling a tube of lipstick from her purse and reapplying in the rearview mirror. "Let alone twice."

"Good point." I thought about that. "But maybe it wasn't the only item Carrington faked. Maybe he did this regularly. Over time, some bigger ticket goods, we could be talking real money."

"Which points more to Van Steinberg than a single buyer," Dana said.

"Another good point." I flipped my visor down, checking my eye makeup as I contemplated that. "So, maybe the buyer of the bracelet finds out she's got a fake and goes back to the auction house she bought it from. Van Steinberg realizes what's going on, and he kills Carrington."

"Over the bracelet?" Dana asked.

I shook my head. "Over his reputation. It might have been a two-thousand-dollar bracelet, but imagine how it would hurt his business if it got out he was auctioning off fakes."

Dana nodded. "Especially if this hadn't been the only time."

"The only problem is, the only buyer I know of is Felix. And he hasn't killed anyone."

"You sure?" Dana teased. She knew better than anyone that our *complicated* past had started off rather rocky.

I gave her a playful punch in the arm. "Yes. I'm sure."

"Well, you know, it's Saturday," Dana pointed out.

I raised an eyebrow her way. "Meaning?"

"Well, chances are Benton's offices are closed."

"And?"

"Well, Benton might not tell you who his buyers are, but he's got to keep records of them, right?"

"Riiight," I said, not liking where this was going.

"What if we slipped in and just took a little peek at them. You know, just to see who might have bought the fake bracelet? Then we could ask her if she told anyone, like Van Steinberg."

"And how exactly do you suggest we just 'slip in'?" I asked.

Dana grinned. "Trust me. I played a cop for three seasons on *Detroit Blue*."

* * *

Life tip: when someone says "trust me," it's usually a sure sign you should *not* trust them.

"How much longer?" I asked, whispering to Dana as she crouched at the keyhole to Benton's offices on the second floor.

"Patience. There's an art to this."

One she had clearly not mastered, as I'd been standing guard in the hallway for at least ten minutes and was getting antsy. We'd spent a half hour in weekender traffic getting to Benton's offices, before casing them out from the comfort of my car. No sign of his Mercedes, no lights in the windows, no sounds beyond the door. After watching for a good twenty minutes, we'd been relatively sure he was out. In fact, most of the offices in the building had a closed look to them, with the exception of a dentist's office occupying the unit closest to the elevators, whose lights were definitely on. It was only a matter of time before someone with a toothache came barreling down the hall, and our jig would be up.

"Are you sure you know what you're doing?" I asked.

"Sergeant Buffy Macintyre did this all the time."

"Why did a police sergeant have to pick locks?" I asked.

"She didn't always play by the rules." Dana paused, glancing up at me. "Tough mom, absentee father. Writers gave her a really compelling backstory."

"Sounds fab," I said.

"It was. No idea why she was canceled, but she was a pro at this."

"But here's a question for you—is out-of-work-actress *Dana Dashel* a pro at this?" I asked.

Dana shot me a look. "I am between jobs. That's not the same as out of work."

"Sorry," I shot back. "Breaking and entering makes me edgy."

"Forgiven," she said, going back to the lock, her tongue protruding from the corner of her mouth at the effort of it. "Now, the key to beating a lock like this is getting all of the pins to release at once. I can get them one by one, but holding them in the right position is the hard part."

Everything about this felt like the hard part. "Maybe this wasn't such a good idea," I said, second-guessing this whole harebrained scheme.

"Just a couple more pins…"

A click sounded, and Dana turned the handle, the door swinging open.

I had to admit, I was kind of surprised it worked. "Wow."

Dana grinned at me. "See? I told you Buffy Macintyre was a pro."

"Forget acting, maybe you should get a job as a real PI," I said, following her inside the office.

"Huh. Maybe I should."

"I was joking."

"Killjoy."

I closed and relocked the office door behind us, happy to have the shield from any dental patients and looked around. The only sound in the room was the bubbling of the fish tank in need of a cleaning.

"Now what?" I asked.

"Where do you think he keeps his client files?" Dana whispered, even though we were clearly alone.

I pointed toward the door marked *Private Office*. "That's the door he came out of when I was here last time."

Dana stepped forward and pushed inside. While the lobby was drab and empty, Benton's private office looked to get a lot more use, clutter covering every available surface. Two bookcases held a hodgepodge of folders, dusty books, and binders. A cheap chrome and faux wood desk held a computer monitor, landline, and a half dozen piles of bills and unopened correspondence. Near the windows a row of file cabinets looked like it hadn't been touched since the cloud had been invented. Two chairs that might have once been for clients, were now serving as host to file boxes, a couple of discarded ties, and an assortment of empty takeout boxes. The entire place smelled faintly of stale cigarettes and kung pao chicken.

"Gross," Dana said, picking through the mess.

"And hardly organized. Where do we start?"

She shrugged, her eyes going to the computer. "There?"

We both crossed to the desk, and I stood behind Dana as she sat in the office chair, the springs creaking under her weight. She jiggled the mouse, and the unit hummed to life, the screen lighting up with a desktop.

Dana clicked around a bit, finding several folders full of files. It seemed that Benton's disorganization extended to his virtual world too, files full of photos mixed with downloaded programs and PDFs, mixed with financial records.

"This guy seriously needs a secretary," Dana decided, clicking another folder marked *important*, which contained two photos of someone's hand covering the lens and one menu from a pizza place.

I shifted from foot to foot, feeling time tick by as she clicked through several more files. I was just starting to give up and contemplate digging through actual paper in the dusty row of cabinets, when Dana opened a folder containing a list of files organized by date.

"This looks promising," she mumbled. She opened a file, and revealed a receipt for an antique that Benton had brokered—a statue of a Greek god, according to the description.

"Wow, this old stuff goes for a lot," Dana said, noting the total for the item that was well into five figures.

"Terri said she saw the bracelet a couple of months ago."

Dana clicked back and scrolled down, finding a date from that time period. She opened the folder, and several files appeared. I felt sweat trickle down my neck as she clicked through each one. The first detailed a sale of a painting, then next an antique merry-go-round horse. Finally the third file held a description of a silver bracelet from the art deco era, purchased for a client at Van Steinberg's Auction House.

"That's it," I said, pulling out my phone and taking a picture of the screen.

"Looks like the buyer was someone named Carla Montgomery." She paused. "Why does that name seem familiar?"

I had no idea and was about to say so, when I heard a sound outside the door. One that sounded a lot like a key being inserted into a lock.

I froze, my eyes shooting to Dana. She stared back at me like a deer caught hacking the hunter's computer.

"What do we do?" she whispered.

"Hide!"

She quickly closed all the computer windows and shut off the monitor as I eyed the door. Nerves built in my stomach, simultaneously making me feel like I had to pee and cry. "Hurry!" I urged.

I heard the outer door open and close, footsteps shuffling across the dingy carpet of the lobby.

I looked around for anywhere to hide. While the room was small, the wall-to-wall clutter looked beautiful now, providing several options for cover. Making a quick decision, I dove behind a couple of file cabinets, stifling a sneeze as a cloud of dust rose in protest.

Dana crouched in the corner, making herself small between the bookcase and the windows.

Just as the door opened and Benton walked in.

I willed myself not to make a sound, not to breathe, not to send out any psychic vibes I was there.

I closed my eyes, listening to Benton move around the room, picturing where he was. I heard shuffling near the desk, the mouse jiggling. A drawer opened, and a moment later I heard what sounded like a pen scratching on paper.

I bit my lip, praying that he was just here to jot down an address or phone number and not to catch up on paperwork for the week.

A few more sounds came from the computer—some pinging as things opened or closed, lots of keyboard clacking, a couple mouse clicks. Finally I heard Benton moving again, the creak from his chair signaling he was standing. Then the desk drawer opened and closed again, and muffled footsteps crossed the room. The door whispered open over the carpet and then shut with a thud as Benton moved back into the outer office.

I didn't dare let out the breath I'd been holding until I heard the outer door close again and the faint sound of a key locking it shut.

I hear a loud exhale across the room to match my own. "Ohmigod, I thought we were caught for sure," Dana breathed, standing.

"Ditto," I agreed, getting up and working a cramp out of my calf. I was pretty darn proud of myself that I hadn't peed my pants while crouching behind the cabinets. "Let's get out of here."

We did, quickly exiting the private office and tiptoeing to the outer door. I peeked my head out. One guy dressed in sweats stood in the hallway outside the dentist's office, drooling slightly as he waited for the elevator. No Bradley Cooper.

"Come on," I urged, pushing the door open. We both slunk out and quickly made for the stairs, clattering noisily down them. I was pretty sure my heart didn't start beating normally again until we were buckled back in my car and I was pulling away from the curb toward the 405.

"Wow, that was invigorating," Dana said once we were safely ensconced in traffic.

The word I might have used was closer to *terrifying*, but I let that go.

"What was the name of the bracelet's new owner again?" Dana asked, pulling her phone out.

"Carla Montgomery," I told her. "Why?"

"I swear I know that name." She typed it into a search engine, scrolling for a couple of seconds before recognition hit. "That's it!"

"What?"

"She's a child psychologist."

"And you know her?"

"No, not personally. But I've heard of her. Remember when that child actress…what was her name…" She snapped her fingers quickly, trying to recall. "Pippi Mississippi! Remember when she had that meltdown in the middle of filming her movie?"

I nodded. "Vaguely."

"She had, like, a TV show where her real life dad played her school principal, and there were dolls and lunch boxes and all kinds of Pippi Mississippi merchandise. Anyway, they were doing a movie to tie in to the TV show, and the teenager had a breakdown right in the middle of it. No one could find her for, like, two days. Then she showed up naked on one of her own billboards, threatening to jump."

"Wow. Sounds like a doozy of a meltdown."

Dana nodded. "It was. *The Informer* dedicated an entire issue to it."

"And Carla Montgomery?" I asked, inching forward in the traffic on the freeway.

"She was the physiologist they called in to talk her down. Only took five hours."

I was about to respond, when my phone rang and Mom's name showed up on my dash display. I quickly swiped her on to speaker.

"Mads! Thank God you're there!"

"Mom, what's going on?" I asked, the panic in her voice immediately putting me on edge.

"It's the police officers. They're here again."

"Laurel and Hardy?" I asked.

Mom paused. "Well, I don't know if they're that bad, Maddie."

"No, those are their names. Laurel McMartin and John Hardy."

"I-I don't know. I didn't ask. It's that man with the goatee and the woman. They say they have a warrant."

"A warrant for what?" I asked, my eyes cutting to Dana. Her brows were pulled down in the same concern I felt flooding my system.

"They said they want to search my car. I don't know what to do."

"Is Ralph there?" I asked, signaling to merge right and exit the freeway.

"No, he's at the salon. But Mrs. Rosenblatt is here with the twins. She says I need a lawyer, Maddie. Do I need a lawyer?"

I hoped not, but I feared the worst.

"I'll be right there," I promised her, exiting on Wilshire and making a right.

Luckily, once I left the freeway, traffic lightened up, and ten minutes later I was pulling up to my mom's place. I parked at the curb next to her mailbox, right behind a nondescript gray sedan with a police light affixed to the dashboard.

The owners of the vehicle were in the driveway, both of them standing over Mom's car, the trunk popped as they rummaged around inside. Mom stood on the lawn in a pair of pleated culottes and a tie-dyed tank top, nibbling on one fingernail. Mrs. Rosenblatt stood beside her, arms waving up and down, shouting a string of curses in Yiddish as her muumuu flapped around her like bird wings.

"*Lign in drerd un bakn beygl!*" I heard Mrs. Rosenblatt direct to Hardy as I got out of my car.

"What does that mean?" Dana asked, the two of us jogging toward Mom.

"I have no idea. Something about a bagel?" I guessed. Though the venom in her voice made the gist clear enough.

"May you burn in hades forever and bake bagels you never eat!" Mrs. R translated with equal venom, spitting on the ground for emphasis at the end.

I still didn't quite get it, but I focused on Mom, grabbing her in a quick hug. "Are you okay?" I asked.

"Oh Maddie!" She hugged back, hanging on tightly.

"It's okay," I said. "Are the twins okay?"

She nodded. "They're inside watching TV. I gave them cookies."

"We'll figure this out," I promised her.

"Yeah, I've already figured out these two are putzes. Putzes, you hear me!" Mrs. Rosenblatt shot toward the duo at Mom's trunk.

Hardy popped his head up long enough to scowl at Mrs. R.

"I'd like to see the warrant," Dana told them. Then she whispered to me. "Don't worry—Buffy Macintyre also went to law school. Almost passed the bar too, before we got canceled."

Oh boy.

I was about to warn her that didn't actually qualify her as Mom's legal counsel, but she'd already approached the two detectives. "Warrant please?" she asked again, hand out.

Laurel straightened up and reached into her jacket, which must have been sweltering in this heat, and handed her a sheaf of papers.

"It says we can search the car and garage."

"For what?" I asked, glancing over Dana's shoulder at the legalese.

"Evidence," Hardy shot back, popping up from the trunk again.

"What exactly do you expect to find?" Dana asked.

"Carpet fibers," Laurel said with a smirk.

"Wait—" I said, thinking back to the night before when we'd found Allison Cash. "You mean you think my mom put Allison Cash in her trunk?"

"You said it. We didn't," Hardy answered.

The two shared a knowing look, as if I'd just confessed.

"This is insane," I said, shaking my head. "What possible reason would my mom have for killing Allison Cash?"

"You tell me," Laurel said, shooting a look at Mom.

Mom's eyes went wide beneath her baby blue eye shadow. "I didn't even know her. I've never met any Allison Cash!"

Hardy opened the rear passenger door of the car and stuck his head inside. "We have a red substance here in the backseat," he said to his partner. "Let's get a sample. Could be blood."

"Blood?" Mom squeaked out, going pale beneath her heavily applied bronzer.

Dana Dashel, counsel for the defense, was at Hardy's side in a second. "Do you have probable cause to take a sample?"

Hardy blinked at her. "What?"

"Isn't this outside the scope of the warrant? Is there legal precedent? Has my client been informed of her rights?"

"Uh…" Hardy looked stumped.

"It looks dried." Laurel crouched to examine the red stain. "Could have been here for some time. A couple days even," Laurel determined, pulling her phone out to take a photo. "Dang it, selfie mode." She clicked a couple of buttons. "Crap, now it's stuck on video. How do you just take a picture?"

"Let me do it," Hardy said, taking his phone out. He pushed a button and talked into his phone. "Siri, take a picture."

A pleasant voice answered from the device. *"Today's starting pitcher for the LA Dodgers is Clayton Kershaw."*

Hardy frowned at his phone. "Not pitcher, Siri. Pic-ture," he enunciated slowly.

"There is a strawberry picking tour five miles from your location."

"I don't want strawberries. Just take a picture of the blood, Siri!" Hardy yelled.

"The Bloods are a notorious Los Angeles based gang," Hardy's phone went on to inform us before he stabbed it into silence with one stubby finger.

I wasn't sure whether to laugh or cry. Instead, I glanced in the backseat of Mom's car through the window.

"That's not blood," I told them, looking at the small stain on the backseat.

Four pairs of eyes turned my way.

"It's fruit punch. Mott's for Tots brand."

Dana snickered. Hardy frowned. Laurel fumbled with her phone to take a note.

And Mrs. Rosenblatt flapped her arms some more. "See, I told you she's innocent, you *schlemiel*!"

CHAPTER FIFTEEN

———

While Laurel and Hardy took their time categorizing whips of nondescript things from Mom's car into plastic baggies, I called Ramirez. Unfortunately, it went straight to voicemail, but I left a message letting him know his colleagues were executing a search warrant on his mother-in-law. While I knew there wasn't a whole lot he could do about it, he could at least check to make sure anything that came in from my mom's car was properly processed. While I didn't think Laurel and Hardy would actually manufacture evidence—one needed an imagination for that—I had no doubt they'd botch it, lose it, or taint it. And the last thing I wanted was for them to come back a second time. I knew the carpet fibers would prove Mom innocent. I just hoped they did it quickly.

Dana and I waited until the detectives had done everything they could to annoy Mom, then finally left. I assured her that Ramirez would take care of everything, as I gathered up the twins and left her in the capable hands of Mrs. Rosenblatt, who promised me she'd spend the afternoon doing an aura cleanse for Mom. While I wasn't entirely sure that was going to help much, Mom seemed comforted by the idea, so I went with it.

Once we got the kids buckled into my minivan and had the AC blasting, Dana turned to me. "We definitely need to talk to Carla Montgomery now."

I shot her a look. "I don't know. Didn't you see those two with a warrant? This is getting real. I'm worried that maybe we should just leave it to the police."

Dana blinked at me. "You're kidding, right?"

I grinned. "Okay, so maybe not *those* police, but I'm sure Ramirez is doing everything he can."

"Sure. Everything he *can*. But I bet we can do more."

"I don't know…"

"Look, it's just a child psychologist's office." She paused, getting a wicked gleam in her eyes. "And we've got the perfect in." She turned slowly in her seat to eyeball the twins.

"You seriously want me to drag my children along to interrogate a potential murderer?"

Dana rolled her eyes. "Don't be so dramatic."

"*Me* the drama queen? Now who's kidding?"

She ignored me, continuing with, "I'm sure Carla Montgomery didn't kill anyone over a two-thousand-dollar bracelet."

"Unlikely," I agreed.

"But, she could very well provide the link we're looking for between the fakes, Benton, Carrington and Cash, and Van Steinberg."

I pursed my lips together, hating to admit she was right.

"We can at least go talk to her," Dana added.

I glanced back at Livvie and Max again. "I guess it couldn't hurt to just go talk to her…"

Famous last words.

Fifteen minutes later we pulled up in front of a tall glass building in mid-Wilshire. After parking in the underground garage, we took the elevator up to the seventh floor, which housed the offices of Dr. Carla Montgomery.

As soon as we entered the waiting room, we were immediately assaulted with the sounds of whining kids, impatient parents, and *Moana* from a TV mounted near the ceiling. The walls were colored in a bright mural of unicorns and dragons surrounding a tall castle, and toys bins and bookshelves lined the walls. Several chairs and a sofa were occupied by parents who all looked slightly harried and tense, and kids who all looked bored and tired. I spied a redheaded boy who I recognized as the youngest sibling on a family sitcom, and a little girl in the corner looked an awful lot like the kid with the scraped knee on a Band-Aid commercial I'd seen recently.

"This place looks expensive," I mumbled to Dana, second-guessing my decisions for the second time that day.

"Relax," she whispered back. "We're just here to talk. We're not actually patients."

"Isn't that what patients do? Pay to talk?"

But she pretended not to hear that as she walked up to the reception desk, where a woman in a pale peach top and headset sat. "May I help you?" she asked in a friendly voice as we approached.

I opened my mouth to speak, but Dana was faster.

"We're here to see Dr. Montgomery about our twins."

I shot her a look. "*Our* twins?"

Dana smiled brightly. "We're a little worried that they're being bullied in preschool. You know, about having two moms." Dana put her arm around my shoulders and squeezed. "Aren't we, honey?"

I forced a smile. "Yes, dear."

"Anyway," Dana said, turning back to the receptionist. "A friend of ours told us that Dr. Montgomery is the best."

"Oh, she is," the receptionist assured us. "Do you have an appointment?"

Dana pursed her lips and frowned. "No, I'm afraid we don't. We were hoping to just meet with her for a couple of minutes and see if she's a good fit for our kids first. Good rapport is so important, don't you think?"

"Uh, yes. Yes, of course." The receptionist turned to her computer monitor. "I'm sure Dr. Montgomery can see you."

"Wonderful!" Dana beamed, sending me a wink.

"Next Thursday," the woman behind the computer finished. "She has an opening at three that afternoon, if you'd like to fill out our new patient intake forms?"

"Next Thursday?" I cut my eyes to Dana. I knew this was a bad idea.

But Dana Dashel, LGBTQ Mom of the Year, was undeterred. "Oh, that feels like a long way off. Is there any way she could squeeze us in for a just a *teeny* moment today?" she asked, holding two fingers up a smidgeon apart to illustrate her point.

"Well, she's awfully busy today..." the receptionist hedged, gesturing to the packed waiting room.

"We'll just be a few minutes. Really. I mean, just to see if the kids take to her?" Dana shot her a bright smile. Then she leaned in confidentially. "Melanie Mississippi told me at brunch the other day that Dr. Montgomery was a miracle worker with her daughter."

"Oh, she did?" the woman said, perking up at the name. "Oh, well, if it's just going to be for a *teeny* moment...let me see if maybe Dr. Montgomery can fit you in between clients. Hang on just a moment, will you?" she asked. She rose from her chair and slipped into a back room.

Dana nudged me. "Never hurts to name-drop, right?"

"Melanie Mississippi?" I asked

"Pippi's mom."

"You don't actually know her, do you?"

Dana shrugged. "I could. I mean, her daughter's agent used to work at the same management company as Ricky's agent's assistant, who introduced me to my last producer. Six degrees or something."

I was about to argue the math there, when the receptionist came back. "Dr. Montgomery is booked full today, but she said if you'd like to meet with her now, she can give you fifteen minutes between clients?"

"Fabulous!" Dana said, clapping her hands. "Max? Livvie?" she called to the twins, who were knee deep in the toy box under the TV. "Follow Mommy."

The kids looked from Dana to me, slightly confused. Then, in toddler fashion, ignored us both, going back to the toys. Finally we each scooped one up and followed the receptionist down a short hallway to an open door.

Dr. Montgomery's office was more adult than the waiting room, painted in warm golden tones. A soft suede sofa took up one end of the room, filled with pillows in pale calming colors. A low table with tiny chairs sat in the center of the room, the top filled with crayons, markers, and coloring pages. The twins made a beeline to it, and I prayed the colors stayed on the paper and not Dr. Montgomery's expensive looking sofa.

A glass and chrome desk sat at the far end of the room, a woman behind it standing as we entered. She was tall, in her mid to late fifties, and wore a loose short-sleeved blouse and dark slacks that ended in pointy-toed heels.

"Dr. Carla Montgomery," she said, extending a hand to each of us.

"Maddie," I introduce myself. "And this is my—"

"Wife," Dana inserted for me, stepping forward to shake the doctor's hand. "Dana."

"Very nice to meet you both," she told us, gesturing to the sofa for us to sit. "And these are your children?"

"Yes," I said, "Max and Livvie. Twins."

Dr. Montgomery greeted them both, though they hardly looked up from their scribbled creations.

"So, what can I do for you today?" Dr. Montgomery asked, taking a chair opposite us and crossing her legs.

"We're concerned about the kids at preschool. You know—how other kids' opinions of their gay moms may affect them," Dana said, her strawberry blonde brows pulling together in mock concern.

"I see," Dr. Montgomery said, nodding sagely. "Have the children expressed unhappiness to you?"

I opened my mouth to say no, when Dana ran right over me with a responding, "Yes!"

I shot her a look.

"Well, they have to me, anyway," she amended.

I shut my mouth with a click. I guess I was supposed to be Bad Mom here.

"I see," Dr. Montgomery said again. "What sort of emotions have they expressed?"

"Well...," I could see Dana trying to come up with something on the fly.

She looked to me.

I just gave her a shrug. Hey, she was the parent who the kids complained to.

"Uh, well," she started. "They ask 'where's Daddy?'"

"At work!" Livvie piped up from the coloring table.

Dr. Montgomery gave me a raised eyebrow.

"Uh, that's what the other kids say," Dana explained. "Their daddies are at work."

"Catching bad guys," Max jumped in.

Dana shot me a look. "Uh, and Max has this delusion that his dad is a superhero." She leaned in to address the doctor. "So sad."

"Daddy's catching bad guys!" Livvie repeated.

"The delusion seems to have spread," Dana said, shaking her head.

"I see," Dr. Montgomery said again, though I could feel the concern in her voice being more directed at my "wife" than the two perfectly well-adjusted kids coloring at the table.

"That's a pretty bracelet," I commented. I gestured to the silver piece of jewelry on the doctor's arm, getting to the point before we ran out of borrowed time.

Dr. Montgomery reached down and twisted the bracelet on her wrist. "Oh, uh, thank you."

"Art deco style, right?" I asked.

She blinked at me. "Oh, uh, yes, actually."

"It's a lovely reproduction," I said, hoping to bait her.

Dr. Montgomery laughed. "Well, thank you, but it's actually not a reproduction."

"Oh?"

"No, 1920s silver and jade. Made by Courtland, actually." She paused. "Antique jewelry is a hobby of mine."

"You're sure it's authentic?" I asked, glancing to Dana out of the corner of my eye.

Dr. Montgomery frowned, as if I'd offended her. "Yes. I'm positive." She took the bracelet off and flipped it over. "See this mark here?"

Dana and I both leaned forward, and I noted a small initial stamped in the silver beside what look like a half-moon.

"Is that a crescent?" Dana asked.

Dr. Montgomery nodded. "It's the mark of Damien Courtland. He went to work for Tiffany in the 1930s, which makes this bracelet more rare than most of its era."

"So this is authentic." I could feel my hopes deflating like a balloon with a pinprick.

"Yes," Dr. Montgomery said, the defensive tone back in her voice as she put the bracelet back on. "I had it appraised for insurance purposes right after I bought it."

"You didn't by any chance use Carrington and Cash for that appraisal?" I asked.

Her frown deepened. "No. Carter House. Why?"

I shook my head. "No reason," I mumbled, all of my neatly lined up puzzle pieces falling to the floor with a crash. Dr. Montgomery had bought a real bracelet at Van Steinberg's auction. But its previous owner had shown Carrington a fake. Had someone replaced the fake with the real thing before delivering it to Dr. Montgomery? Which made no sense—usually real items were switched out for fakes, not the other way around. Why would anyone substitute a fake item for a real one?

"…opening to start therapy next week."

"What?" I glanced up, realizing Dr. Montgomery had been talking.

"I really think it's best we start sooner rather than later." Dr. Montgomery glanced at Dana. "Maybe even start with family therapy."

"Sure, right," I said. "Uh, we'll have to think it over."

"Yes, well, please call my office if you'd like to schedule that intake appointment," Dr. Montgomery said as we pried the twins from the coloring table. Max whined in protest, and in the end I think Livvie smuggled a crayon out with her.

Once we had them buckled back into their car seats and the AC was blasting the interior of my minivan again, Dana turned to me.

"I don't get it. The bracelet is real."

"Apparently," I said. I didn't know how hard it would be to fake a silver art deco bracelet, but if Carla'd had it independently appraised after the auction, I was inclined to believe it was the real deal.

"So now what?" she asked.

I glanced at the dash clock. 3:00 p.m. "Now I take these two home for a nap and hope they don't tell Daddy about their two mommies."

Dana grinned at me. "And my agent said I couldn't play lesbian."

* * *

Once we got back to my place, Dana took off to pick up the napkins and tablecloths for Ricky's party, and I went into nap negotiation mode with the twins. It was a hard sell after the excitement of the afternoon, and it took three bottles, two bedtime stories, and one lullaby sung slightly off key, before they were both out. I celebrated by doing the dishes, starting a load of laundry, and tidying up the living room, all while trying to rearrange the bits and pieces of information I'd picked up over the last few days.

Either Carrington was selling fake antiques and swapping them out at some point—why I couldn't fathom—or our Clown Lady, Terri Voy, was the fake. Either way, someone was lying. And I was pretty sure almost everyone involved knew more than they were saying. Well, everyone but me, who felt more and more clueless the more I learned.

I was wallowing in that disconcerting thought, when my phone rang.

From somewhere.

I glanced around the living room, trying to discern where the sound was coming from. After checking under the sofa, behind the TV, and in the dishwasher, I finally found it shoved into a snow boot by the back door just as it was about to go to voicemail. Apparently Max had been busy before his nap.

"Hello?" I said, quickly taking the call.

"Hey, it's Ricky."

"She's not with me," I told him.

"Huh?"

"Dana?" I said. "She said she was with me today, right? Like, shoe shopping or getting a pedicure or something?"

Ricky chuckled softly on the other end. "Actually she said she was taking you to the gym."

"And she expected you to buy that?" I asked with a laugh. Dana had long ago given up on me doing anything that resembled exercise. While she was as dedicated to her workouts as I was to coffee, my idea of cardio was power shopping in three inch heels.

"Actually, I was calling to ask you a favor," Ricky went on.

"Me?" I asked. "Okay, shoot."

"I have a little surprise of my own planned for Dana. I'm going to spring it on her at the party."

"Wait—*you* have a surprise planned for Dana at *your* surprise party?" I wasn't sure she was going to like this. "What kind of thing are we springing on her?"

"I can't tell you."

"Why not?"

"Because you're a terrible liar, and Dana will find out."

I rolled my eyes in the empty living room. "Fine. So what's the favor?"

"I have a couple people I want to make sure are on her guest list. But I don't know how to contact them. I was hoping you had their addresses?"

"Who?"

Ricky rattled off a few names, including Dana's aunt in Palm Springs and one of our mutual friends from junior high.

I frowned at the phone. "You want these people at *your* birthday party?" I asked.

"It's important that they be there for the surprise I have for Dana."

I shrugged. "I guess I can dig up that info."

"Great! Just text it over to me, and I'll take it from there."

I agreed, hoping I wasn't getting in over my head as I hung up.

* * *

The twins woke up from their naps early, and feeling like I'd been an absentee parent lately (and just a little guilty for involving them in our interrogation), I took them for a walk to the neighborhood park before setting them up with a tub of blocks in the living room and contemplating dinner options. Chinese takeout was sounding like a viable one, as Ramirez walked in the front door.

"Hey," he said, only pausing for a quick kiss on my cheek before making for the fridge and a bottle of beer.

"That kind of day, huh?" I asked, leaning against the counter.

He grunted in response, sipping deeply.

"Couldn't have been worse than my mom's," I told him.

He paused mid-sip. "How is she?"

"Rattled."

He shrugged. "Laurel and Hardy have that effect."

"Please tell me you were able to run interference."

He sighed. "Honestly, babe? I've been trying all day. Carpet fibers are with the lab, though I doubt they'll get much." He paused. "Sorry you got my voicemail. I was with forensics when you called."

I raised an eyebrow his way. "And?"

"And what?"

"And what did you learn at forensics? It was about Carrington's case, right?"

He narrowed his eyes, clearly debating how much to tell me.

"Come on. You can't leave me hanging." I paused. "I'll pick up moo shu pork for dinner," I said, trying on bribery.

"Done." The corner of his mouth quirked upward. "Report came back on the type of weapon used to kill Allison Cash."

"And the weird casings?"

Ramirez nodded. "Hardy was right. They were weird. Antique, to be exact."

"Antique!" My mind immediately went to Yesterday's Treasures and the glass case filled with antique weapons I'd seen when I'd first visited. "Any idea what kind of antique weapon they're from?"

"Very good idea," Ramirez said, nodding. "Smith & Wesson single-action revolver."

"Is that one of the weapons at Carrington and Cash's antique shop?"

"Not sure yet. Forensics just published the report, so *if* Laurel and Hardy are doing their jobs—"

"That's a big *if*," I mumbled.

"—they should be checking any weaponry either victim owned."

"Wouldn't the gun be registered?" I asked.

He shook his head. "No need to register weapons made before 1899. They're considered historical pieces, not firearms."

"Even if they still shoot real bullets," I mused.

He nodded. "ME found two in Allison Cash."

I cringed. While everything I'd learned about the woman so far had been less than flattering, no one deserved that.

"Mom does not own a Smith & Wesson," I said.

Ramirez set down his beer. "Which is the first piece of good news we've had yet." He paused. "Shall we celebrate by ordering that moo shu?"

* * *

I was sitting in a dark room, and I could just barely hear someone calling my name. It was like a far off whisper, and as much as I strained to hear it more clearly, it eluded me. I blinked my eyes, trying to adjust to the absence of light, but blackness was all I saw. Then I felt a chill. Cold enveloped me, wrapping around my arms like an icy embrace.

"Who's there?" I called out in to the dank, dark nothingness. But only the whisper came back, still calling my name. It was as if someone was trying to tell me something, trying to reveal themselves to me. It was someone I knew. But recognition was just beyond on my grasp.

"Who are you?" I yelled, feeling frustration grow inside of me.

But the only thing I heard back was the soft voice calling, "Maddie? Maddie?"

It was like it was taunting me, purposely staying just outside my reach.

Suddenly a sound broke through the quiet. Loud music, jarring, shaking me.

I blinked, sunlight suddenly pouring into my consciousness as I realized I'd been dreaming. And the loud music that had awakened me was my phone, calling irritatingly from my nightstand.

I fumbled, glancing at the time as I moved to silence the ringtone. 6:15 a.m. Way too early.

"Hello?" I croaked at whoever had the nerve to call me this early.

"Mads, it's me." Faux Dad's voice came over the line.

I blinked sleep out of my eyes, as the urgency in his tone jolted me awake. "Ralph? Is everything okay?"

"No, Maddie, it's not."

Ramirez stirred beside me. "What's going on?" he murmured.

I shrugged. "Ralph, what's going on?" I was fully awake now.

"The police showed up again," he said, his voice cracking. "Only this time they didn't just ask questions. They arrested your mom for murder!"

CHAPTER SIXTEEN

———

By the time I had thrown on a pair of jeans and a T-shirt and shoved my bed head under a baseball cap, Ramirez was up, making coffee and calling his captain to find out exactly what had happened. Several swear words were thrown around as he got the details that Laurel and Hardy had arrested Mom based on the carpet fibers in her car being a match for those found under Allison Cash's fingernails. Which meant that, like Mom, the killer had driven a Toyota with beige carpeting. Along with thousands of other people in LA. It was hardly a smoking gun, and apparently Laurel and Hardy had known that, as they'd waited until the night judge was on to get the warrant signed. Possibly even exaggerating a few of the details of the case in the process. And waiting until Ramirez was off duty to execute the warrant. With the way Ramirez's eyes were flashing as he relayed that part, I almost felt sorry for the two.

Almost. They *had* arrested my mom.

Ramirez promised to drop the kids off at his mom's before going in to the station, and I jumped in my minivan and took off for the county jail, where Mom had been booked.

I found Faux Dad in a sad waiting room full of plastic chairs, crackling fluorescent lights, and other worried looking family members awaiting arraignments for their loved ones. Faux Dad looked like he hadn't slept in a week, and his eyes were red and wet with tears. I held his hand as we waited for Mom's case to come up, and after arranging bail via a bond for which Faux Dad bravely put up Fernando's as collateral, we waited what felt like another eternity for Mom to be released.

Her normally fluffy feathered bangs drooped in unwashed strands across her forehead, her eyeliner was smudged, and it looked like she'd cried off most of her mascara. Instead of looking cheery, her hot pink T-shirt and stonewashed jeans looked rumpled and too bright to compete with the slump to her shoulders and dirt smeared across the top of her white Keds.

I bit back tears and hugged her fiercely. If Laurel and Hardy had been anywhere near me in that moment, *I* would have been the one Mom and Faux Dad would have needed to bail out of jail.

"Are you okay?" I asked, the question sounding ridiculous given the circumstances.

Mom sniffed and nodded bravely. "I met some very interesting people this evening."

I barked out a laugh through my tears. "I bet you did."

I followed Mom and Faux Dad home, seething the entire way, and made sure Mom was tucked into her bed with a warm cup of tea, a soft blanket, and about a million reassurances that Ramirez was doing damage control and would take care of everything.

Reassurances that sounded hollow even to my own ears but, along with a Valium, they seemed to put Mom's fears to rest at least long enough for her to get a nap in.

I was leaving her place when my phone rang with Marco's face on the screen.

"Honey, Ralph left a message he's not coming in to the salon today. What happened?" he cried as soon as I picked up.

"They arrested Mom last night." The words felt like lead in my throat.

"No! Not Betty!" Marco gasped on the other end. "Is she okay?"

I nodded into the phone as I got back in my car. "She's sleeping now. But she's been through it." I felt that anger rising again as I filled Marco in on the details.

"So what do we do now?" Marco asked when I'd finished.

"She's out on bail, and Ramirez is looking at what he can do to refute the so-called evidence."

"Well, that's great, but what I meant is, what can *we* do?" Marco clarified.

"We?"

"Honey, I don't know about you, but I'm not just gonna sit on my gorgeous behind while your mom is being carted off to jail!"

Despite the morning I'd had, I couldn't help grinning at his loyalty. "Thanks." I paused. "And you know what? You're right."

"Dahling, I'm always right."

I glanced at the time on my dash clock. Bailing Mom out had taken most of the morning. "I've got to pick up my check at Van Steinberg's Auction House this afternoon," I told him. "But I have a couple of hours to kill before then."

"I say we kill them interrogating that shopgirl about the fake antiques."

"Mina?" I frowned.

"Uh-huh. Look, the only other two people who handled the items at Yesterday's Treasures are dead. If something funny was going on at that shop, she must have known about it."

"I guess it's worth a try," I decided.

"Great! I'll meet you there!" Marco promised.

I was about to tell him I could handle it on my own, when he added, "Oh, and I have the invitations."

"What invitations?"

"The ones for the people on Ricky's invite list. He said you'd have addresses for them?"

Mental forehead thunk. "So you know that Ricky knows about the party too?"

Marco *tsked* on the other end. "Honey, when will you learn that Auntie Marco knows all?"

"Okay, so tell me—what's this surprise within a surprise that Ricky has set up for Dana?"

"Sorry, doll, no can do. Ricky has sworn me to secrecy."

"Please?" I pleaded.

"No way. It's against the party planners' code to squeal."

"You do not have a code."

"Maddie, if I tell you, Dana will know the second you open your mouth. You are a terrible liar."

"I am not a—"

"What is that?" Marco cut in. "Mads, you're breaking up..."

"I'm not breaking up. I can hear you fine."

"You must be going over Laurel Canyon again. I can hardly hear you."

"I'm not going over—"

"I'll meet you at the antique shop," Marco sang into the phone, then hung up on me.

* * *

Fifteen minutes later I pulled up outside Yesterday's Treasures. I took a minute to assess my reflection in the rearview mirror. Unshowered and not totally rocking the casual chic look, I took off the ballcap and tried to fluff my hair a little while I waited for Marco. I quickly threw on some mascara, eyeliner, and lip gloss, hoping to detract from the small stain I now noticed on the white T-shirt I'd thrown on in my haste to leave the house. I was just capping my tube of Raspberry Perfection when Marco's mint green MINI Cooper pulled up behind me and he waved in the mirror.

As I got out of the car, Marco gave me a quick head to toe and clucked his tongue. "Honey, we can do better than this."

"I left the house in a hurry," I mumbled, tucking my hair behind an ear.

He cocked an eyebrow at me. "I have never been in *that* much of a hurry."

I took in his pink denim short shorts, rainbow colored cap sleeve T-shirt, and purple platform shoes. "I think you're fashion enough for both of us."

He tossed nonexistent hair over one shoulder. "I know."

I resisted an eye roll and led the way into the antique shop, listening to the bell chime above the door as we pushed inside.

As with my previous visits, the amount of interested clientele had once again grown with the shop's notoriety. Several people browsed among the goods, while others took selfies and whispered in hushed tones about murders.

Mina stood near the register, deep in conversion with another patron. At the sound of our approach, both turned, and I realized I knew the patron—Terri Voy, our Clown Lady.

Terri blinked at me behind her large glasses. "W-what are you doing here?" she demanded. "Are you stalking me?"

I couldn't help the laugh that escaped me. People who lived in glass houses shouldn't throw clowns.

"Terri, this is Maddie Springer," Mina said.

"I know who she is. She was at my house yesterday. And the day before." Terri crossed her arms over her chest. "And I'm starting to think you're not with the police."

Smart cookie. "I'm helping them"—sort of—"looking into the deaths of Peter Carrington and Allison Cash."

Mina's eyes immediately hit the floor at the mention of her *two* deceased employers. "I can't believe Allison is gone too. Terri and I were just talking about that when you came in."

"Oh?"

Terri nodded. "Tragedy."

Though I noticed no signs of the grief she'd displayed at Carrington's passing in her eyes now that it was Allison's dead body we were discussing. She glanced past me, eyes resting on Marco.

"Are you with the police too?" she asked, skepticism clear in her voice.

"Only the fashion police, dahling. I'm Marco," my companion said, sticking his hand out toward Terri. "Charmed, I'm sure."

Terri shook his hand lightly, as if slightly blinded by the outfit. I didn't blame her. It could probably be seen from space.

"Was there something I could help you with?" Mina asked.

"Actually there was," I said, shifting my attention to her. I decided to be blunt and lay it all out on the line. "I wanted to know about the fake art deco bracelet that Carrington auctioned off at Van Steinberg's."

I watched Mina's reaction carefully, but if she knew anything about the fake, she didn't let on. Instead, her eyebrows drew together in a deep frown. "Fake bracelet? No." Mina shook her head. "No. Like I told the police, everything I've seen here is authentic. I'm sorry, but you must be mistaken. Mr. Carrington would never do that."

I turned to Terri, who had become distinctly quiet during our little exchange. "Am I mistaken?" I asked her pointedly.

Terri's magnified eyes went from me to Mina. "I-uh…"

"You told me you saw him appraise it, here in the shop."

Terri's mouth opened and closed a few times, as if trying on different answers before finally settling on the right one. "Y-yes. I did."

Mina sucked in a breath. "What did he say? When was this?" she demanded.

Terri licked her lips. "A couple months ago. You were on a lunch break, and this woman came in. Peter looked at the bracelet and said it was a reproduction."

"And he offered to buy it from her?" I asked.

Terri nodded. "Yes. But just as costume jewelry. I think it was something like a hundred dollars."

"Well, then it must have been a reproduction," Mina decided. "Mr. Carrington didn't make mistakes."

"So how come it sold for two thousand dollars in an auction just a couple of weeks later?" Marco cut in.

"N-no. No, it must have been a different bracelet," Mina protested.

I looked to Terri again.

"Sorry, Mina," she said in a quiet voice. "But it was the same one. I'd swear it. Silver and jade. I didn't want it to be true either. But it is."

Mina frowned again. "I don't believe it." But this time some of the fight had gone out of her words. I watched her, confusion and disappointment warring on her features. If she was acting, she was doing a bang-up job of it.

Then again, this *was* Hollywood.

"You didn't know anything about this?" I pressed her.

"No!" she said hotly. "Of course not."

"And Allison Cash?" Marco cut in.

"What about her?" Mina asked. Her posture had gone decidedly defensive since we'd walked in the door.

"Did Allison know Carrington was selling fakes?" I asked.

Mina shook her head, her hair whipping back and forth. But she paused a couple of shakes in and bit her lower lip. "I-I don't know. I would never have guessed Carrington would do such a thing, but…I honestly just don't know anymore."

"What about records?" I asked. "Would Carrington have recorded his purchase of the bracelet? Or the sale?"

Mina nodded. "Sure. But Allison usually handled all the paperwork."

"Do you have access to it?" I asked.

She nodded. "Allison's cousin called this morning. He said he'll be flying in to take over the shop next week. He gave me all the passwords and everything to keep it up and running until then."

"Any chance you could look for the records of the bracelet? It was made by Damien Courtland."

Mina nodded again, all fight having left her. "I'll just be a minute," she said, and disappeared into the back.

I glanced over at Terri, who I noticed had gone quiet again at the mention of records. Though, she didn't look in a hurry to leave as we stood at the glass case waiting for Mina to come back. She wandered over to the shelf of antique dolls, running her hand over one's hair, straightening the pinafore on another.

We didn't have to wait long, as Mina reappeared from the back with a printout in hand. "I found this." She handed the paper to me. "A Courtland, purchased on the 6th and sold at Van Steinberg's on the 23rd."

I glanced at the page, noting there was no mention of the purchase price or selling price. No name for the women he'd bought from and no mention of his buyer, Carla Montgomery. I felt my hopes sinking. Nothing here indicated what Carrington's scam had been or how and why he'd swapped the fake-for-real bracelets.

Or who had killed the appraiser and his partner.

CHAPTER SEVENTEEN

———

After thanking Mina for her time, we left the shop, leaving the tinkle bell over the door in our wake as we walked back to our cars. Marco begged to tag along to Van Steinberg's to pick up my Chanel shoe check, so we left his MINI Cooper at the shop and took off in my minivan.

The parking lot was sparsely populated today, nothing being put up for public auction. I pulled into a spot near the front, and we both braved the hot few steps from the AC in my car to the AC in the auction house. The hushed vibe of the place was even more pronounced today with an absence of the bidders and chatter that had accompanied my last visit here. The slim woman behind the reception desk told me Van Steinberg was in his office, expecting me.

"Ms. Springer," he greeted me as we stepped inside. He was dressed in his usual attire of a smart suit, polished shoes, and a necktie. His gaze flickered to Marco's short shorts as I introduced my friend, but Van Steinberg was thankfully too polite to say anything.

"Pleasure to meet you," Van Steinberg told Marco, shaking his hand.

"Ditto. I've heard so much about you," Marco said.

"Oh? Well, yes, thank you. We do a brisk business here, so it's nice to hear that our reputation precedes us. I have your check ready," Van Steinberg went on, gesturing for us to sit in the club chairs opposite his desk. We did, and he opened a drawer and extracted an envelope with my name on it.

"I'm sure you've heard about Allison Cash's death by now," I said, trying to figure out how to delicately approach the subject.

Van Steinberg paused. "Uh, yes. Very sad. Whole affair is quite tragic."

"Did you know her well?" I asked.

"Uh, no. Not really. Carrington was the one who did most of the auction work."

I nodded. "Yes, you had mentioned she was more of the businesswoman behind the operations."

He smiled and nodded. "Yes, that's correct."

"So, you don't think she knew about the fake antiques Carrington was passing off?" I tossed out as bluntly as I could for shock value.

Van Steinberg blinked at me, his white mustache twitching. "Excuse me?"

"Carrington," Marco jumped in. "He sold an item at one of your auctions that was a fake reproduction."

"I-I-I don't know what you're talking about!" Van Steinberg's pallor went from pale to pink as he sputtered. "That's preposterous. The idea of such a thing! That's quite an accusation, young lady," he directed at me.

While I appreciated the "young" part, his tone was anything but complimentary. "I know for a fact that Carrington put an item he appraised as fake into one of your auctions," I said. I pulled the record Mina had given me out of my purse, pushing it across the desk to him. "Two months ago. This Courtland bracelet. Benton won the auction for his client Carla Montgomery."

Van Steinberg opened a drawer to his right, extracting a pair of glasses that he perched on his nose before examining the document. "Yes, yes, I do remember this bracelet." He set the paper down. "But I can assure you it was not a knock-off."

"How can you be so positive?" Marco pressed.

"I examined it myself. It had the maker's mark on the inside, and everything about it was the right age, weight, and style."

"But Carrington told the original owner that it was a fake," I protested.

"What was a fake?" a voice came from the doorway.

I spun in my seat to see Lottie, the collector who'd sold The Blob, standing in the doorway. Today she was dressed in a paisley printed polyester shirt that looked like she'd ripped it off of Carol Brady. She'd coupled it with a brown corduroy skirt that clung in all the wrong places, and a large tortoiseshell clip holding her dyed orange hair. Her heavily made-up eyes were narrowed in concern as she looked from Van Steinberg to me, her false eyelashes blinking up a storm.

"Nothing was fake," Van Steinberg answered her emphatically.

Marco spun around in his seat to face the woman. "It's possible Carrington was passing off reproductions as real antiques," he said all in a rush.

"But not through my auction house, I assure you," Van Steinberg said. "Every item he sold through here was 100% authentic." He paused, handing me the envelope with my name on it. "I believe our business here is done. Now, if you'll excuse me, I have a payment to process for Ms. LaMore here."

Effectively dismissed, Marco and I stood, mumbling our goodbyes to Lottie, who still looked a bit perplexed at the entire thing.

I had to admit, she wasn't the only one.

"So Carrington swapped out the fake bracelet for a real one *before* selling it at auction?" Marco asked as we got back into my car.

I shrugged. "Or else Van Steinberg is lying about it being real."

"Or," Marco said, "Terri Voy has been lying this whole time about the original appraisal."

I was turning that thought over as Marco's phone rang—singing out Cindy Lauper's *Girls Just Want to Have Fun.*

He looked down at his readout. "It's Dana."

"Put her on speaker," I said, turning the car on and pulling away from the curb.

"Hey, girlfriend," Marco answered, singsonging into the phone as he held it flat in his palm.

"Don't you 'hey' me!" she shouted back. "I'm at the address you gave me to go over the menu. And I'm not amused, Marco."

I raised an eyebrow at him. That didn't sound good.

"Wh-what do you mean?" Marco asked, blinking innocently at his Android device.

"I mean," came Dana's angry voice, "this is *not* the Asian street fair themed menu I approved."

Marco shrugged. "I upgraded it."

"Crickets?" she yelled. "Crickets are an upgrade?!"

I barely stifled a laugh.

"Is that Maddie with you?" Dana asked.

Okay, maybe I didn't entirely stifle it.

"I'm here," I confirmed. "He's serving guests crickets?" I shook my head at Marco.

He shrugged in mock innocence. "They are delightful. So trending. Very exotic."

"They are bugs," Dana argued.

"Delicacies!"

"Where are you?" Dana demanded.

I glanced at a passing street sign. "Just passing Olympic in Century City."

"Great. You can be here in ten minutes."

I glanced at my dash clock. "Uh, actually, I was…"

"Get. Here. Now." And Dana hung up.

Marco let out a long sigh. "Wow, talk about ungrateful. I mean, you know what I had to do to get fresh crickets flown in from Thailand?"

I blinked at him. "You do hear yourself, right?"

"Just drive." He slunk down in his seat.

While part of me wanted to tell him to clean up his own mess, the bigger part of me definitely did *not* want cricket a la mode for an appetizer.

So, exactly twelve minutes later, we were walking through the doors of Bugging Out, an "exotic insects" bar in Beverly Hills. While the décor was sterile, modern, and gleaming white, the air held a faint scent that reminded me of the bait shop my uncle had brought me to when I was ten. Behind the bar stood a guy in a white chef's outfit and a man bun, trying to calm one very unhappy strawberry blonde in stilettos. At the sound of the door opening, Dana spun, immediately homing in on Marco as her eyes narrowed to angry slits. "*There* is my party planner," she ground out.

Man Bun looked very relieved. "Ah. Yes. As he can tell you, we have an order prepaid for two-hundred cricket croquets.

I stifled a gag reflex.

"Prepaid," Dana repeated, still death-glaring Marco. "Without asking me."

"You said money was not an issue," Marco replied, blinking back at her with his best innocent face—eyes wide and rimmed in black liner, extra-long lashes fluttering up and down.

"Well, I didn't think you'd use it to buy bugs!"

"Exotic edible insects," Man Bun corrected.

Marco nodded, gesturing at the man. "See? They're all the rage."

I bit my lip to keep from cringing as I perused the menu. Deep fried grasshopper, bee larva frozen yogurt, silkworm smoothie. I could see why this was popular among the Beverly Hills set. One look at the menu, and you'd lose your appetite for a week. Best diet ever.

"…we can substitute the crickets for something else." I tuned back in to Man Bun's negotiations.

"What kind of something else?" Dana hedged.

"Yes!" Marco agreed. "Okay, maybe the crickets were a bad idea," he conceded.

"Ya think?" Dana shot back.

"Maybe we should go with something a little more classic. How about dung beetles?"

"Gross! No, I will not have my waiters serving guests beetles!"

Marco rolled his eyes. "Well of course waiters won't be serving beetles."

Dana's shoulders relaxed a scooch.

"We're having the appetizers served by drones."

Dana's head whipped around so fast that I swore I could feel the wind. "Drones?"

"Isn't it fabulous! I mean, what more trending way to receive your exotic appetizers than via flying drones?"

"There is no way—"

"Of course, they may scare the burros." Marco paused, thinking this one through.

"You still haven't canceled the donkeys, you ass—"

"But I'm sure they'll be stabled by their handlers by then. I mean, the drones don't come out until the West African dancers have cleared the floor."

"African dancers?"

"*West* African," Marco corrected. "There is a difference, you know."

Dana's face was a shade of pink I'd only seen achieved by Mary Kay. Her mouth moved up and down, but no words came out. If I had to guess, nothing she was thinking was appropriate for polite ears. Very restrained of her, really.

"Oh, gee, look at the time," I said, checking my phone. "I've got to go pick up the twins. Dana, you can drop Marco off on your way home, right?"

"Maddie?" Marco turned a pleading look to me.

"Maddie!" Dana sent me an entirely different look. One that had a lot more fire. And maybe even a little murder behind it.

"Good luck," I told the erstwhile party planner as I hightailed it out of the bug bar. Before someone fed me a grasshopper.

* * *

Crisis averted(ish), I took side streets toward home, letting my mind wander back over what I'd heard from Mina, Terri, and Van Steinberg that day. Unfortunately, I felt like the more I found out, the less I knew about who could have killed Carrington and Cash. But Marco had brought up a good point about Terri Voy. The truth was, so far, everything I found said that Carrington had been selling real antiques. Felix's sculpture was real. Carla's bracelet was real. Van Steinberg said he'd checked for authentication himself. In fact, everyone except Terri seemed sure Carrington was selling the real deal. Which left me with Terri herself. Had she lied about Carrington telling the owner the bracelet was fake? If so—why? Was she trying to hurt Carrington's reputation posthumously? While Terri seemed a bit unstable to me, I'd had the distinct impression she was telling the truth about what she'd seen Carrington do. She had every reason to protect him and none to disparage him.

So if Terri wasn't lying…who was?

I was so deep in thought that I'll admit I wasn't 100% paying attention to the other drivers on the road as I pulled off the 2. Traffic was moving along at a decent clip, even if we weren't yet hitting the speed limit. The car in front of me was going at a steady pace, and I was zoning out much of the rest— billboards passing without really seeing them, cars going by in blurs of dents and rust, trucks making the occasional shadow as they pulled alongside me.

I vaguely registered a car pacing me in the next lane over, just in my blind spot. Which I honestly barely noticed until we rounded a corner and the sun peeked between the buildings to glint off something shiny and metallic in the window of the car beside me.

Then a crack rang through the air, the window behind me shattering on impact.

CHAPTER EIGHTEEN

———

Shards of glass rained down on me, spraying my backseat and embedding in my hair. I heard a scream that I vaguely registered as coming from me, as I instinctively swerved right, away from the other car. Horns honked in protest behind me, and I fought to get the wheel under control, tires squealing with the effort.

Another loud crack rang out, this time followed by a metallic ping as something embedded itself into the side of my minivan.

Someone was shooting at me.

I'd heard of these things happening in LA before, but I'd never been the victim of a drive-by myself. I swiveled my head to the left, but the sedan had slowed down, moving a car length behind me. I could tell it was gray, late model. I could make out a figure in the driver's seat, but features evaded me.

I stepped on the gas, surging ahead and looking for somewhere to pull off the road. The sedan surged in answer, coming up beside me again. Close enough that I could look directly through the windows at the driver. He or she was dressed all in black, and a ski cap totally covered the person's face. Man, woman, young, old, black, white—all I knew was that they were intent on me as they raised the gun, pointing it right at me.

I screamed again and slammed on the brakes, my car swerving to the right with the force of it. I fishtailed back and forth, struggling to regain control. Horns honked behind me again, and I watched the sedan sail past my window, flying down the road as I finally careened to a stop, slamming into a parking meter at the curb.

I breathed deeply, foot still jammed on the brake, not daring to let go. Cars continued to zoom past me on the street, as if nothing had happened, completely ignoring the minivan with a bullet hole in the side that was parked halfway up the sidewalk. I ignored them right back as I took stock.

My back window was toast, pieces of it scattered throughout the interior. I noticed a few small cuts on my bare arms and hands, still gripping the wheel with all my might. I could see the front end of my car tilting the parking meter at an odd angle and knew that was going to cost a pretty penny to fix—both the car and the money I'd owe the city for the damaged meter.

But at least I wasn't dead.

I'm not sure how long I sat there before the shock started to wear off and my brain clicked back on. Finally I put the car in park, shut off the engine, and fumbled in my purse for my phone. My hands were shaking so badly that it took me two tries to get Ramirez's number up on the screen before I finally heard it ringing. I said a silent prayer that it didn't go to voicemail.

"Hey, beautiful," he answered.

"Hey yourself," I responded.

But my usual greeting must have sounded as shaky as I felt, as his tone instantly changed—the easy affection replaced by concern.

"You okay?" he asked.

"Yeah," I lied. Then I looked around the car. "Actually, no." I licked my lips. "I think I was just the victim of a drive-by."

"What?!" I could hear movement, like Ramirez rising from a chair. "What happened? Are you okay?"

"I'm fine," I said. "Shaken up, but I think I'm okay." I paused, taking a deep breath. Just hearing Ramirez's voice grounded me a little, and I drew some strength from it. "I was just pulling off Santa Monica when someone shot at my car."

I heard more movement—keys jangling and footsteps. "Where are you?" he asked.

I looked up and rattled off the cross streets.

"Don't move. I'm on my way."

Don't worry—I wasn't sure I could move even if I wanted to.

I waited what felt like an eternity before I finally grew restless and got out of the car, assessing the damage from the outside. A small, perfectly round hole sat in the middle of my sliding back doors. My heart kicked up a notch, just thinking about what would have happened if the kids had been in the car with me. Livvie's car seat was filled with glass shards. I felt tears pricking my eyes at the terrible juxtaposition of such violence against such innocent reminders of my sweet babies.

I swiped at them as I spied Ramirez's black SUV down the road, lights flashing on the dash and traveling at speeds that would make a CHP officer pull out his ticket book with glee. He pulled to a slightly more graceful stop behind me than I'd managed, scarcely waiting until the engine was off before jumping from the car. In a second he was at my side, wrapping me in a big bear hug that made those tears threaten again.

I hugged him back, not ever wanting to let go. His hands stroked my hair, his lips going to my forehead.

"You've got glass in your hair," he murmured.

"I've got glass everywhere," I told him as I pulled back.

His dark eyebrow drew together in concern. "What happened?"

"I-I honestly don't know. It all happened so fast." I sucked in another deep breath, trying to calm my nerves enough to recount the details. "I was driving along, when my window just suddenly shattered. I didn't realize what was going on until they shot again and hit the side of the car." I gestured to the bullet hole in the door.

I could see Ramirez clenching his jaw, anger building. "They? Did you get a look at the perpetrator?" he asked, going into Cop Mode.

I shook my head. "He was wearing a ski mask," I told him. Then I added, "Or she. I-I really couldn't see anything."

"What about the car?"

"A gray sedan?"

"Make? Model?"

"I-I don't know. It all happened so fast," I repeated.

He let out a long breath. "Don't suppose you got a license plate number?"

I shook my head. "By the time I got the car under control, they were gone." I paused. "Sorry. I'm a lousy witness."

Some of the cop softened out of his face, and he pulled me in for another long hug. "I'm just glad you're okay," he murmured into my hair.

"Me too," I told his chest as I pressed my face to it.

"This is going to be a mess to explain to the insurance company," he said, clearly trying to lighten the mood.

I pulled back, taking in my battered car. "And I don't think this was a random drive-by," I said slowly, watching my husband's reaction.

His jaw did some serious clenching again, working back and forth. "That's concerning," he finally ground out.

I bit my lip. "I, uh, think it might be connected to Carrington's death."

Ramirez took a step forward, crouching down to get a closer look at the bullet hole in my car. "Should I ask why you think that?" he said.

"I may possibly have been asking some questions today. To some people who knew him."

"Questions." His tone was flat, but I could see that jaw working again. This time it was accompanied by a small vein in his neck bulging ever so slightly.

"Look, I was in public places. Out in the open. With Marco even!"

He stood, turning to face me. "Six inches in the other direction, and the bullet would be in your chest."

The fear I'd been attempting to quell ever since my window shattered hit me in a wave, reminding me how lucky I'd been.

I could see the same emotion in Ramirez's face too as he took a step toward me. "Maddie, this is a murder investigation. This is not some game."

"I'm well aware. *I'm* the one who was shot at, remember?"

While I expected a fight back, his face softened instead. "That is not something I ever want to hear again."

I swear his voice cracked on that last line.

Tears gathered in my eyes again. I sniffed them back. "I know," I choked out. "Me neither."

He pulled in a deep breath, nostrils flaring at the effort. "Look, I am doing everything I can to get your mom out of Laurel and Hardy's sights. Against Captain's orders, by the way."

I reached a hand out and grabbed his. "Thank you."

"You're welcome. But I need you to stay out of it."

I bit my lip. While all my feminist instincts screamed to tell him that wasn't his call, my better judgment knew he was right. Just how close I'd come to being a statistic on the evening news had hit me hard. What would Max and Livvie do if something happened to me? It wasn't just myself I had to look out for anymore.

So, I nodded, fully meaning it. "I'll leave it to you."

I must have shocked my husband as much as I shocked myself, as he cocked an eyebrow at me. "Really?"

"Really," I assured him. "I trust you. You'll find whoever did this," I said, gesturing to the car, "and killed Carrington and Cash."

He nodded, still looking me as if he didn't quite believe me. But he said, "Thank you. And, I *will* find them."

I glanced at the car door. "You think the same weapon did this that killed Allison Cash?"

"Too soon to tell." He crouched down at the hole again. "I can see the bullet was small caliber, but we'll have to dig it out and compare the two to know for sure."

I cringed at the words "dig it out."

"My car is evidence now, isn't it?"

Ramirez gave me a sympathetic smile. "Sorry, babe. I'm going to have to call it in and have them tow it."

While it wasn't ideal, I was still on a high of just being alive, so I only groaned minimally as I grabbed my purse and personal belongings from the car. Ramirez called in the incident, requesting a forensics team, before taking the car seats out of my minivan, shaking the bulk of the glass off of them, and transferring them to his own vehicle. We only had to wait a few minutes before a black and white squad car arrived, pulling to a stop just behind Ramirez. He gave the uniformed officer a brief rundown on the situation then left him to await the forensics team.

The drive home was quiet and thankfully quick. I wasn't sure if it was the sleepless night, the early morning call from the prison, or the ebbing adrenaline leaving me drained, but I was suddenly exhausted, every muscle in my body feeling limp and used up by the time we pulled up to our bungalow. Ramirez walked me inside, where I promptly went into the hottest shower on record. By the time I'd gotten out, done a little lip gloss and eyeliner routine, and dressed in a comfortable pair of loose palazzo pants and a cropped shirt, I found Ramirez in the living room, just ending a phone call with someone.

"Car's at the station, and they'll be working on a bullet match soon."

I nodded, hoping they found something useful and my ordeal might not be for nothing.

"You okay?" he asked.

I gave him the best smile I could muster. "I'm good. Really."

I must have been getting better at lying, as some of the concern smoothed from his forehead. "Good. In that case, I'm going to go pick up the kids from my mom's. I've already called Dana to come hang out with you while I'm gone."

"I don't need a babysitter," I told him, sinking into the sofa.

"Too late. She's already on her way." He shot me a big smile. "Be back in a few minutes. If you're real good, I may even stop for pizza on the way home."

"No fair. You know my kryptonite."

He gave me a knowing wink before ducking out the front door.

Left alone, I settled on the sofa and flipped on HGTV, watching a couple in Iowa decide between three gorgeous houses for sale at prices that would make anyone on the West Coast jealous. They were just leaning toward the two story colonial, when my phone rang and an unfamiliar number came up on the screen.

"Hello?" I answered.

"Hi. Maddie Springer?"

"Yes?" I asked, expecting the pitch of a telemarketer to come next.

"This is Lottie. Lottie LaMore. I, uh, got your number from Mina at Yesterday's Treasures."

"Lottie," I said, sitting up straighter. "Hi. Is everything okay?"

"Yes, yes. I just…well, I was thinking about what you said at the auction house earlier today. About Carrington and falsifying antiques."

"Oh?" Lottie had been a regular at Carrington's shop. Had she, like Terri, witnessed Carrington selling fakes as well? "What about it?" I asked.

"Well, there's something I think you need to know."

"Yes?"

She paused, and I could sense hesitation on the other end. "I-I'd really rather discuss it in person. Is there any way you could meet me?"

"Now?" I asked, glancing at the clock. Despite how drained I felt, it was only late afternoon.

"The sooner the better in this case, I think," she said. "I…well, I think it might be important."

I bit my lip, my angel shoulder and devil shoulder doing an internal battle. I'd promised Ramirez I'd stay out of the whole case less than an hour ago. And unlike the past times I'd made that same vow, I'd fully intended to keep it this time. But if Lottie knew something about Carrington…something she was willing to share with me…it might well be the key to making all the bits and pieces I'd been chasing down over the last week fit into neat little places.

"Maddie?" she asked.

"Sorry, uh, yes. Where would you like to meet?" I asked, mentally planning the apology dinner I'd owe my husband now.

She gave me the address to her house, and I promised I'd be there as soon as I could.

CHAPTER NINETEEN

———

I was just throwing on a pair of red heels and an extra layer of lip gloss when Dana arrived a few minutes later. I met her at the door, pulling it open almost as soon as she knocked.

"Mads! Ohmigodyoupoorthing!" she slurred together, attacking me with a linebacker worthy hug.

"I'm fine," I protested. "But you might be breaking a rib."

She let me go, shaking her head in disbelief. "Ramirez said you were a drive-by victim! What happened?"

"I'll tell you all about it in the car."

"Wait—what?" Dana asked as I grabbed her by the arm and shoved her back out onto the front porch.

"We're going to visit Lottie LaMore."

Her blank face told me the name didn't ring a bell.

"The antiques collector who sold The Blob sculpture."

"Oh." She nodded, recognition dawning as I locked the front door behind me and headed to the car.

As I buckled in, I sent Ramirez a short text telling him I was with Dana and we were making a quick little trip to visit a friend. Then I shut my phone off for fear of the texts I'd get back.

"So, why are we going to see Lottie?" Dana asked, backing her car out of my driveway.

I quickly told her about the phone call from Lottie, then as we hopped onto the 10 freeway, bravely recounted the entire shooting incident.

When I'd finished, her usual perfectly smooth forehead was puckered in concern, and her lips were drawn into a tight line. "You got too close to the truth, Mads," she decided. "That's why the killer tried to take you out."

I shivered despite the heat wave. "I only wish I knew what that truth was."

"Maybe Lottie's story will help," Dana said, merging onto the 110.

I hoped so. Because I was running out of options.

A few minutes later we pulled up to a one story ranch house in south Pasadena. Dana parked at the curb, and I shielded my eyes from the sun as I stepped out into the heat. The grass looked in need of a good mow, but the roses leading up to the door were bright and well pruned, and while the stone pathway looked worn in places, it was weeded and well cared for.

After beeping the car locked, Dana followed me up the walkway to a front door that was painted a cheery red, and I rang the bell.

Lottie must have been waiting for us, as I'd barely heard the chime sound on the other side before the door pulled open.

"Maddie, I'm so glad you could make it." She paused when she saw Dana. "And you brought a friend?"

"My car's in the shop," I said, glossing over the details. "This is Dana. I believe you met her at the shop?"

"Yes. Of course, I remember you now. Please, come in." Lottie stood back to allow us entry.

The interior of the house was cooler, thankfully bathed in air conditioning, and I was immediately struck by how much Lottie and her late husband had packed into the small home. A living room sat to our right, where three large, overstuffed love seats were rammed in between several end tables in a mix of styles—all of them dating back at least a few decades. The floor was covered in several rugs in competing designs, and the walls were adorned in paintings, photographs, and various items framed in shadow boxes, almost creating a second layer of wallpaper over the floral design that was already pasted up. Ahead of me was an entry hall that I presumed led to back bedrooms. It, too, was covered in a hodgepodge of décor from yesteryear.

"Wow," Dana said, mirroring my thoughts as she took in our surroundings. "This is quite a collection."

"Thank you." Lottie nodded, the pride apparent on her face. "But my husband was the one who collected most of these. He used to say he was rescuing history."

"That's lovely," I said, meaning it. While the mishmash of stuffy furniture wasn't my taste exactly, I did appreciate the craftsmanship and stories they had to tell. Speaking of which…

"You, uh, said you had something to tell me about Carrington?" I prompted.

Lottie cleared her throat, her expression morphing from serene to troubled. "Yes. Uh, why don't we step into the study and chat there? I just made some iced tea."

I nodded, and Dana and I followed her down the hallway toward a small room that had been fashioned as an office. Three of the four walls were lined with bookcases featuring all manner of antiques, from books with well worn spines to sculptures to groupings of tin toys and porcelain figures. A desk sat at one end of the room and a sofa and small coffee table in the center. As with the living room, the floor here was covered in old rugs—so many that some overlapped in places.

"This was Louis's favorite room," Lottie said, her eyes taking on that faraway look again. "See that knife over there?" she asked, pointing to a rusted looking bowie knife beneath a frame. "That was his first antique purchase. Picked it up at a rummage sale as a young man. Paid just ten cents for it, and later found out it's worth several hundred dollars. He was hooked after that."

"Super cool," Dana said, taking a step closer to examine it under the glass frame.

Lottie chuckled. "Yes, well, I suppose it is cool. Excuse me just a moment while I get the tea."

"Can you imagine if each of these things is worth a few hundred dollars?" Dana asked, moving on to a shelf holding an assortment of pottery pieces. "Lottie could be sitting on a fortune here."

"I wonder how many of these were purchased from Carrington," I mused.

Dana shrugged. "Or if they're all authentic."

I didn't have much time to ponder that, as a moment later Lottie came back, carrying three glasses on a tray, along with a plate of cookies. She set it down on a small coffee table in the center of the room and offered a glass to me. "Peppermint brewed with a hint of raspberry," she said. "Very refreshing for these warm days."

"Thank you," I told her, taking a sip. She was right—the peppermint added an extra cooling component.

"And for you, my dear," she said, crossing the room with a glass for Dana.

Only she must have tripped on the edge of one of the layered rugs, as she stumbled toward my friend, the glass in her hand pitching forward.

And spilling all over Dana's white linen skirt.

Dana gasped and jumped back.

"Oh no! Oh, I'm so sorry!" Lottie said, hand going to her mouth in embarrassment.

"It's okay," Dana reassured her. "Cold, but okay."

"No, I-I'm so clumsy sometimes. Here, let me take you to the powder room, where you can clean up."

Dana shot me an eye roll before following Lottie out the door to the restroom. I had a bad feeling I owed her an apology dinner too, for dragging her along.

I sipped my own iced tea in the silence for a couple of moments, browsing the room. In one corner I found a pair of sculptures very much like The Blob, only a bit larger and...well, uglier. I picked one heavy lump of clay up, turning it over in my hand to see a small signature on the bottom: *Bracington*.

"My Louis purchased that in the eighties," Lottie told me, coming back into the room. "It's quite rare to find a pair still together like that "

"It's...very nice," I said, setting the indistinguishable shape back on the shelf next to its mate. "You mentioned something you needed to tell me about Carrington?" I prompted again, feeling a little uncomfortable in the claustrophobic space.

Lottie bit her lip and nodded, turning to the tray again as she grabbed her own glass of tea. "Yes. I believe I do."

"Did you ever see him trying to sell items you thought might be fake?"

With her back to me, I couldn't read her expression, but her voice held a note of sadness when she spoke again. "I had such faith in Carrington. You see, my husband had been dealing with him for years. He trusted him to know the difference between something valuable and something just old. Louis had a great eye for history, you know," she said, turning to face me. Her lips held a sad smile, and her eyes seemed to focus on a point somewhere in time rather than in the room. "He saw beauty and craftsmanship, but that didn't always equate to a valuable piece in the antiques world. Condition, rarity, provenance. Those all matter far more, and I'm afraid my Louis never really did develop a knack for differentiating between history and value."

"Well, he seems to have amassed a large collection anyway," I said.

Lottie nodded. "Oh, he did." She paused. "And he trusted Carrington to give a fair price when he was ready to sell them."

"He sold a lot to Carrington?" I asked.

Lottie's expression changed, the faraway look being replaced with something else I had a hard time reading. "He did. More than he should have."

"Meaning?" I asked.

But instead of answering me, Lottie set her tea back down on the tray and said, "Did you know it can be almost impossible to tell a reproduction from the real things sometimes?" She didn't wait for an answer before continuing. "Old materials are easy to find, thanks to the internet, and a clever forger can duplicate almost any marks or insignia. In fact, to an untrained eye, a reproduction and an authentic piece can look almost identical."

"That sounds difficult," I agreed.

"It is. Which makes people like Carrington so important. People we trust to tell us what we have in hand. People who know the difference between pretty junk and real valuables." She paused. "At least when they tell the truth."

Now we were getting somewhere.

"Did Carrington lie to you about a reproduction? Did he tell you it was real?" I asked.

She shook her head. "No, dear. That wasn't the lie he told."

"But he did lie to you about the value of an item," I said, feeling pieces slowly fall into place as I watched her face. "He lied to you about a *real* antique, didn't he?"

Lottie sucked in a breath, eyes intent on mine as she slowly nodded.

"Carrington wasn't selling fakes," I said, clarity washing over me almost like a physical thing. "He was selling real antiques...but he was telling the people he bought them from that they were fake."

Lottie's eyes were watery as she nodded. "I'm afraid so."

I thought back to when I'd first met Carrington at the *Antiques Extravaganza.* "Just like he did to Mom's hatpin," I said, working it out. "She was sure it was real, but he told her it was a cheap reproduction. That was his scam. He'd tell owners they had junk, offer to buy it off them for a small sum, and then resell it at auction for the real money it was worth."

Lottie sighed deeply. "See, I knew you'd figure it out."

Something about the tone of her voice pulled me out of my own thoughts. "You knew what?"

"The moment you mentioned fakes at Van Steinberg's, I knew you were getting close to what Carrington's real business was. And it was only a matter of time before you realized why he was killed." She paused. "And by whom."

I blinked at her, the meaning behind her words slow to sink in. Though, as soon as she opened a drawer to her right and pulled out its contents, the meaning was crystal clear.

Just as clear as the shiny antique gun in her hand.

I swallowed hard.

"Lottie? What are you doing?"

She sighed again. "Only what needs to be done, dear."

Panic surged through me as she took a step toward me. "*You* sold Carrington antiques," I said, almost more of a statement than a question.

Lottie nodded slowly.

"Ones that he told you were reproductions. And bought off you cheap."

She nodded again.

"And you killed him over it?"

"He killed first!" Lottie shouted, her voice suddenly filling the space. "He killed my Louis."

"Wait—Carrington killed Louis?" I asked.

"When Louis realized that Carrington had duped him, it broke his heart. He couldn't believe he'd been taken in by such a charlatan…that he'd given away his collection for nothing when it was worth so much more." She sniffed, her eyes going watery again. "Louis had a heart attack three weeks later. And it was all his fault."

"So this was about revenge?" I asked, my eyes on the gun. Honestly, at this point, I didn't care what it was about. All I cared about was that gun trained on me. And while I knew it was old, I also had a sneaking feeling it still fired well—well enough to ping my car and shatter my back windows. I didn't want to know what it would do to me.

"It was about justice," Lottie said vehemently. "It was about Carrington getting what he deserved."

"Look, let's just put the gun down and talk. Dana's going to walk back in here any second, and when she does, she's going to call the police and…" I trailed off as I watched Lottie's expression go from anger to amusement.

And reality hit me.

"Dana's not coming back in here, is she?"

Lottie shook her head back and forth, a wicked smile laughing at me.

"What did you do to her?" I asked, panic surging through me anew. I'd never be able to live with myself if anything happened to her.

"Don't worry about your friend. She's taking a little nap in my bathtub right now."

"Nap?" I squeaked out, hoping that wasn't code for something more sinister.

"It was a bad idea bringing her here," Lottie scolded me. One of my worst.

"But you'll both be in a happier place soon."

I swallowed hard. I had a sneaking suspicion she didn't mean Disneyland. "You can let us go," I tried. "We won't tell anyone."

"Now, Maddie, we both know that's a lie. I can't let you live now," Lottie said, matter-of-factly, as if she were telling me she couldn't let me wear white after Labor Day. "You know too much, dear."

The irony was that up until she'd pulled out her gun, I'd known zilch. If she'd just left it alone, chances were she'd have gotten off scot-free.

Then again, if she had her way, there was still that possibility.

I tamped down another surge of panic mixed this time with a healthy dose of desperation as I tried to keep her talking. If she was talking, she wasn't shooting. And anything that was not shooting sounded great right about then.

"How did Louis find out Carrington had given him false appraisals for his antiques?" I asked her, eyes scanning the room for anything I could use as a weapon. Porcelain figures, small toys, framed paintings. Everything felt delicate and light.

"That was Allison's mistake," Lottie informed me. "Louis overheard her bragging to Mina about how much Carrington had gotten at a recent auction for a Tiffany lamp."

"And Louis had sold the lamp to Carrington?"

She nodded. "Carrington had told him it was worthless. Mass produced junk!" She spat the words out, anger rising again. "Louis was disappointed to hear the lamp wasn't real, but he trusted Carrington. We both did."

"What did Louis do?"

"Nothing," Lottie said, her eyes misting again. "When he realized he'd been conned, he was too devastated, too humiliated. Do you know how many pieces he sold to Carrington?"

I shook my head, eyes darting around the room for an escape route. A window stood to my right, but even if it hadn't been sealed with a rusted screen on the outside, it was too high to jump through. Lottie stood directly in front of the doorway. I could try to rush her, but with a gun in her hand, I didn't like my odds.

"My husband sold Carrington dozens of items," Lottie went on. "A good portion of them deemed 'junk' by that crook Carrington. That man had made a killing off my poor Louis's good nature."

"And then Louis died," I said quietly.

She nodded. "But I couldn't let him get away with it," Lottie said, menace clear in her voice.

"What did you do?" I asked.

"I waited," she said. "I brought antiques to his shop, went to auctions he worked. I wanted to see him for myself, lying, cheating, duping good people."

"And you were waiting for an opportunity to kill him," I finished for her.

She nodded. "When I saw him try to pull his same act on your mother, I knew he had to go. He was so smug. So above everyone else. The way he dismissed your mother with a lie. I had no doubt he'd planned to find her later and offer to take that hatpin off her hands. It was only his bad luck that she stood up to him."

"And you saw your opportunity."

"I did." She paused. "I'm sorry your mother had to be involved, but her argument with Carrington was just too perfect."

As far as apologies went, that one was pretty lame. But, considering she had me at gunpoint, I let it slide, instead trying to keep her talking. "You followed my mom to the food court."

"I did. At first, I honestly followed her just to tell her the hatpin was probably real. To have it appraised somewhere else. But when she got up and left her purse sitting there, that sharp little pin right on the top…well, as you said, I saw an opportunity and took it."

I licked my suddenly dry lips. "And you went after Carrington?" I asked, thinking of the false eyewitness report that someone had seen my mom with Carrington right before his death. I realized now it must have been only half false…they hadn't seen my mom, but they *had* seen an older woman with Carrington—Lottie.

She confirmed my suspicions by nodding. "I found him in the back room. I said I needed to speak to him about a piece of jewelry I'd brought in. The second he leaned over to examined it…" She trailed off, and I could well imagine the scene.

"You killed him."

"He deserved it," she spit out. "He killed my Louis, and he deserved to die."

"And Allison?" I asked. "Did she deserve to die too?"

Lottie scoffed. "All Allison cared about was the bottom line. She turned a blind eye to what he was doing because he was making profits for the business hand over fist."

"That day I met you at the shop. The day after Carrington was killed. You were there to see Allison," I said, the timeline becoming clear.

Lottie nodded. "I had no intention of selling her the Dilama sculpture—it was just a way to get in the door. To see how much she really knew about what her business partner had been doing for years."

"You confronted her at Yesterday's Treasures?"

"I did." Lottie straightened her spine, pulling herself up to her full height.

"What did she say?" I asked.

"She laughed," Lottie said, her eyes narrowing. "Can you believe it? That chit had the nerve to laugh at me. She said Carrington hadn't done anything illegal—that I could prove. He'd done—what did she call it?—*shrewd* bargaining. She said it wasn't her fault if old fools believed him. Fools. How dare she call my Louis a fool!"

I could see Lottie's color rising as the monologue went on, could see her reliving the scene in her head. I wasn't sure whether that was good or bad for my current situation, but I instinctively took a small step backward, coming up against a bookcase.

I felt around with my fingers behind me for anything sharp or heavy enough to use as weapon but came up empty.

"Allison was just as bad as Carrington was," Lottie said, continuing her tirade. "It was clear she knew what had been going on, and didn't care."

"So you killed her too?"

"It wasn't hard. I sweet talked Mina into giving me Allison's address, and I showed up at her house later that evening. She was surprised to see me, of course, but she let me in."

"I'm guessing the gun persuaded her?" I asked, eyes on the weapon. It certainly had a way of making me pay attention.

Lottie laughed, her smoker's hack making it come out in a throaty, menacing tone. "Yes, she wasn't expecting that, was she?"

"Why did you move her body to the park?" I asked, shifting to my right to feel along the top of a smaller bookcase. I felt my hopes surge as my hands encountered something small and metal. Though, as my fingers surreptitiously explored the object, it was not, as I'd hoped, a letter opener or small pocketknife but instead a spoon. Dull. Round. Totally useless against a gun.

"I had to make sure the police stayed focused on your mother," she stated simply. "If Allison was found too quickly, I knew it would be easier to pinpoint exactly when she'd died. And it would be more likely your mom could provide a viable alibi. But the longer the body sat, the harder it would be for the police to narrow down the time of death."

I frowned. That was actually pretty clever. "How did you know that?"

She blinked at me. "Well, I read crime novels of course. Doesn't everyone know that?"

Mental forehead thunk. "So you put her body in your car?"

"Yes, that was difficult," Lottie said, nodding. "For a small woman, Allison was surprisingly heavy. I supposed that's why they call it dead weight, huh?" She grinned at her own joke. "But, once I rolled her onto a bedsheet, she was easier to drag out the side door to the driveway. And after I backed my car up to the door, it was just a matter of hauling her up into the trunk."

"And you dumped her in the park?"

She nodded. "I thought about driving farther...up into the hills or someplace, you know. But, well, it's just not safe in places like that after dark for a woman alone these days."

I resisted the urge to roll my eyes at the murderer who was afraid of being out alone after dark.

"It was you on the road today too, wasn't it? In the gray sedan and the ski mask."

Lottie clicked her tongue. "It was frightfully hard to see out of that thing. I was lucky I didn't crash!"

"Gee, lucky you," I mumbled.

"What was that, dear?"

"Nothing," I quickly covered.

"Hmm." She narrowed her eyes at me again for a beat before continuing. "Anyway, it was all working splendidly, the way those police officers were looking at your mom. I heard she was even arrested."

She had a pleased look in her eyes that caused anger to mix in with my fear and panic. This woman had killed two people, sent my mother to jail, shot at me on the road, and now done who-knew-what horrible thing to Dana. My patience was wearing thin with her.

And, I realized as she took a step toward me, my time was running out.

Lottie shifted her stance, holding the antique gun straight armed in front of her. "I am sorry it's come to this," she told me. "But it's time for you and your nosey friend to disappear."

"Don't you think the police will come looking for us?" I asked. Desperation was a physical sensation now, churning in my belly in nauseating waves.

"Oh, I'm sure they will." Lottie smiled, lined red lips stretching over her yellow teeth in a predatory grin. "But no one will think to look for you *here*."

Unfortunately, she was right. I hadn't told Ramirez where I was going for fear of the wrath of Bad Cop. But right then, all I wanted was for Bad Cop to show up. Preferably before she shot at me.

But I realized as she took a threatening step forward, no Bad Cop was coming to my rescue. No Marco, no Mom, no Faux Dad. No posse from the *L.A. Informer*. I was on my own.

And I was not ending this way.

I took a deep breath, shoving fear down as far as I could and doing the only thing I could think of to throw her off balance.

I screamed.

I let out the loudest, sharpest, most ear piercing scream I could muster, channeling my twins when they didn't get their way with just about anything.

And it had much the same effect on Lottie as they did on me—sensory overload that resulted in just a second of confusion.

But a second was all I needed.

I grabbed behind me for anything I could get my hands on and threw it toward Lottie's head. The spoon sailed through the air, not doing much damage as it pinged off Lottie's side. I grabbed and tossed again, firing a string of small porcelain bunnies toward her head.

"Ow! Stop it!" She pulled the trigger as she ducked, a shot ringing through the room before embedding itself in the ceiling.

I dove to the right, throwing myself behind one of the love seats. I heard the crack of the gun go off again, and a tuft of fabric flew into the air.

"No!" she cried. "Look what you've made me do. That was an eighteen hundreds William Morris print!"

I didn't wait for her to regain her aim, shoving my shoulder into the back of the love seat and lurching it forward. It caught Lottie in the shins, sending her reeling backward into the coffee table, where iced tea and cookies splattered on the floor.

Before she could get her balance, I threw myself forward at her in a tackle.

The gun waved my direction, and I landed on top of Lottie just in time to change its direction a half inch as it went off again, taking out a chunk of plaster from the opposite wall.

I grabbed her arm, trying to pry the gun from her hands. But anger and adrenaline had made her freakishly strong. Her white knuckles had the gun in a death grip.

"Let go of me!" she yelled. She lifted her head toward our arm wrestling match, and before I could register what was happening, sunk her teeth into my hand.

I cried out, instinctively pulling back.

Which gave her the upper hand with the gun, as she struggled to a sitting position to aim at me again.

With my injured hand, I lunged forward, trying to grasp at anything I could. My fingers connected with her hair, and I yanked with all my might.

Only as she scrambled away from me, the hair came right off, and I realized I was holding a wig.

"My hair!" she cried, her free hand going to the fine wisps of gray hair that were matted to her head. "How dare you!" she screamed.

She'd been able to not only scoot away from my grasp but also regain her footing. She pointed the gun at me as I sat on the floor in a puddle of iced tea and cookie crumbs, holding her hair in one hand.

"You wicked, wicked, girl," she seethed, breathing heavily through her teeth. Her nostrils flared, her chest rose and fell in her paisley polyester shirt, and lipstick was smeared across one cheek in a grotesquely crazed look. She narrowed her eyes at me, held the gun out in front of her, and aimed straight at me.

Time stopped. All sound disappeared, all thoughts emptied from my head, and I swore I even felt my heart cease beating for that one terrifying second.

I steeled myself for the force of the bullet as I heard the gun cock.

But instead of the crack of a bullet, I heard the sound of a thud, then a grunt, and Lottie fell unceremoniously forward, crashing into the coffee table again.

All the air rushed out of my lungs as I looked up to find Dana standing in the doorway, a large Bracington blob of a statue held in one hand as a weapon.

I guess modern art was good for something after all.

CHAPTER TWENTY

———

I sat outside on Lottie's front porch, giving my statement to a young officer with a buzz cut who'd had the unfortunate luck of being the first one on the scene. After I'd liberated the gun from Lottie's hand and Dana had made sure she was still breathing, we'd called 9-1-1, who'd promptly sent Officer Buzz Cut to us, along with EMTs who were currently trying to revive Lottie while Buzz Cut's partner read her rights. Buzz Cut had ushered Dana and me out to the porch to take our statements, but I wasn't sure either of us had been able to give him a clear version of the events yet.

Apparently as soon as Lottie had "accidentally" spilled the iced tea on Dana, she'd led her into the bathroom, where she'd hit her over the back of the head with a bathroom scale then tied her up with duct tape and left her in the bathtub. It had only been when Dana had heard the first gunshot that she'd come to and realized Lottie was nuts. She managed to pry the tape off her ankles and wrists by the time she'd heard the last shot, and she'd crept into the room unseen and grabbed one of the sculptures to knock Lottie out from behind.

For which I would be forever grateful.

I was just detailing again for Buzz Cut the confession Lottie had made to the murders of Carrington and Cash, when a familiar black SUV screeched to a halt at the curb, parking crookedly. As soon as the engine went off, the driver's side door flew open, and Ramirez jogged toward me.

As much as I thought of myself as a strong woman, I dissolved into tears the moment his comforting arms were around me. All of the fear, panic, and desperation I'd held in while confronting Lottie came surging out in a flood of hot, salty tears that I couldn't stop if I wanted to. I was in full blown hiccup sobs by the time he pulled back and let his dark eyes rove my body in an assessing sweep.

"Are you okay?" he asked slowly, as if trying to break through my hysteria.

I hiccupped and sniffed loudly. "I think so."

He ran a hand over my hair in a tender gesture. "Liar," he whispered.

One more sob escaped me, but I forced a smile along with it. "Physically, I'm fine. Bruised hand," I said, holding it up.

He frowned. "Did she have a dog?"

I shook my head. "No. She bit me."

He shook his head, his expression dark. If Lottie wasn't already in handcuffs, I might have feared for her life in that moment.

"I'll live," I assured him.

"You'll need antibiotics," he decided.

"But I'll live," I repeated, focusing on the positive. Those three little words hadn't seemed so likely a few short minutes ago.

Ramirez must have realized the importance behind them too, as he hugged me fiercely again before calling one of the EMTs over to look at my hand.

Over the course of the next hour, more officers showed up, more EMTs, some guys in CSI jackets, and trailing along behind them all, Laurel and Hardy. I credit the type of man my husband is that he didn't even gloat once as he filled them in on how his wife had elicited a confession for them. As they hung their proverbial heads in shame, Ramirez also made sure they would drop all charges against my mom ASAP.

By the time my hand had been treated and bandaged, the lump on Dana's head had been examined, and Lottie had been escorted to the hospital, handcuffed to a gurney, the sky was dark and my body was limp with exhaustion. Ramirez had one of the officers drive Dana home and another follow them in her car before bundling me into the passenger seat of his SUV.

I must have dozed off a bit on the ride home, as it seemed instantaneous. I jolted awake as his engine cut out in our driveway. I let Ramirez open my door and lead me inside, where nothing but quiet greeted us.

"Where are the kids?" I asked, the silence a foreign sound in our home.

"As soon as I got the call, I dropped them off at your mom's."

I raised an eyebrow his way. "Visits to two different grandmas in one day?"

"I know. They're going to be spoiled beyond belief when we finally get them home."

"Maybe we could hold that eventuality off a little bit longer?" I said.

Ramirez grinned down at me as I stepped into his open arms, feeling warmth radiate off him in calming, familiar waves that instantly rejuvenated me. "What did you have in mind?" he murmured seductively into my hair.

"A hot bath and a soft bed."

He chuckled, the deep rumble vibrating through me as he held me close, sending heat through my body.

"And maybe a little adult snuggling," I added.

He pulled back just enough for me to see the wicked gleam in his deep brown eyes. "You had me at bed."

* * *

I had to hand it to him—Marco had outdone himself. And that was saying a lot, considering it was Marco we were talking about.

From the moment I stepped into the large outdoor patio of the venue Marco had rented out for Ricky's birthday party, my eyes hadn't known where to land—glitz and glamour practically dripping from every detail. And yes, I did *walk* into the party. No burros. I guessed Dana had finally won that battle. There were, however, live peacocks strutting around the party guests, their bright plumes elegant against the backdrop of little black dresses and dark colored suits. Hundreds of tiny fairy lights danced above us in a large canopy, almost like little stars in the sky. Tables were covered in tasteful silk cloths, a quartet played soft jazz music in the corner, and outdoor heaters provided a warm ambiance to stave off the crisp breeze that had decide to blow in just for the occasion, signaling the end of our Southern California heat wave.

"Looks like the kid pulled it off," Ramirez remarked beside me, accepting a glass of champagne from a passing tray.

I nodded in agreement. "Who knew he could do tasteful?"

Ramirez chuckled into his glass as I grabbed myself a champagne glass too. Though, I declined the passing tray of appetizers. Something dipped in chocolate, but until I was 100% sure it didn't have six legs, I was sticking with sparkling wine.

Ramirez guided me toward the jazz quartet with a hand at the small of my back. I'd dressed in a lavender colored satin spaghetti strap dress in a simple mid-calf length that showed off my silver stilettos, and his hand was warm through the thin fabric. We joined the rest of the partygoers, whom Marco had corralled into place for the big reveal when Dana approached with Ricky.

Ricky's secretly invited guests mingled near the lawn, as well as Mrs. Rosenblatt, who sported a fancy muumuu made with two sided sequins that kept changing color as her arms brushed her sides. Mom and Faux Dad stood just to her left, Mom in a floral dress that looked like it was from the Laura Ashley catalogue of 1989, and Faux Dad in an outfit I halfway suspected he stole from Liberace's closet.

"Shhh," Mom told me in a giddy whisper as we approached. "They'll be here any minute." She shot me a wide grin rimmed in matte baby pink lipstick, and I didn't have the heart to tell her Ricky was already in on the surprise. I was glad, though, to see her back to her old happy self.

As promised, all charges against her had been dropped as soon as Laurel and Hardy had returned to the station. I'd never known those two to do paperwork so fast, but I understood why—Ramirez's Bad Cop face was a mighty influencer in that department. While Mom's hatpin had to remain in evidence, at least through Lottie LaMore's trial, she had felt some vindication that, with all the media attention after Lottie's arrest, Van Steinberg had contacted her to tell her he recognized the gems in the murder weapon as part of Josephine Bonaparte's private collection…and it was worth quite a bit more than just the price of the silver.

Van Steinberg's interest in the media might not have been idle curiosity, as in the wake of Carrington's death, the *Antiques Extravaganza* had called him to fill in their recent vacancy for on-air talent. Word was he'd be the newest resident appraiser as their show took to the road in the new season. Apparently he didn't mind those flea-market-Sally groupies quite so much if they were to be grouping around him.

The other venture left in the lurch at the demise of both Carrington and Cash was Yesterday's Treasures. Mina had called me when the news broke of the arrest, and filled me in on Allison Cash's cousin, who'd flown in to decide the fate of the shop. Though, when he'd seen the number of customers who'd been flocking in since the media attention, he'd decided to not only keep the doors open but also appoint Mina as a partner to run the shop for a share of profits. Something she'd been more than happy to do—though this time she'd make sure the profits on the shops' books were put there the right way.

According to Mina, one of the many antiquers who had flocked to the shop in the wake of the press was Johan Burdorf, the famous German maker of dolls—and clowns. Terri Voy had been so starstruck to meet him that she'd even got him to appraise her jewel buttoned, harlequin dressed porcelain clown she'd taken to the *Extravaganza*. Mina said poor Johan made the mistake of asking to see the rest of Terri's collection. I had a feeling the German clown maker would be seeing a lot more of Terri, as the new object of her affection—or obsession, as the case may be.

As it turned out, Benton had been blissfully innocent in the murders and the fake antique scheme, as he'd told Cameron Dakota, in an exclusive interview for the *L.A. Informer*, he'd "always suspected" something was a bit off with the provenance he'd received with items originating from Carrington. Benton's familiar good looks had helped the interview video go viral, and Benton's phone had been ringing off the hook with business so much since that he'd raised his commission rates. Much to Felix's chagrin, as he'd bemoaned to me later, deciding that the stock market might be less volatile than the antiques market after all.

"Places, everyone! They're valeting the car!" Marco said, running in from the entrance in a pale pink tuxedo and waving his arms in the air.

All murmured conversation ceased as we stood as quiet as a hundred people in evening dress could, all eyes on the entrance. A couple of beats later, conversation floated to us from the pathway as Dana and Ricky approached.

"…not sure why you chose this place, but it sounds lively," I heard Ricky tell Dana.

"Oh, it is!" she said. "Just right through here…"

The couple came into view—Ricky in a smart looking navy suit and Dana in a long white cap sleeve dress—and the room erupted as one.

"Surprise!!"

Ricky blinked, grinning wide as he put a hand to his heart in mock shock.

Dana beamed, looking like she'd just pulled off the moment of the decade. "Happy birthday! Did you have any idea?"

Ricky shook his head. "No clue. Wow, you really pulled it off!" Though, as he gave Dana a hug, he winked at me behind her back.

I raised a glass in acknowledgment, relieved I could stop pretending to everyone about not knowing anything.

As the night went on, I drank more champagne than I had intended and ended up thoroughly enjoying some of Marco's flamboyant touches throughout the evening. The *West* African dancers were actually spectacular, putting on a colorful, lively show that got the whole crowd up on the dance floor. The Asian street fair food was delicious, and I gorged myself on mango sticky rice and curried prawn. And while I did hear one waiter describing cricket-dusted chicken skewers to a guest, most of the canapés were insect free. And only one plate was delivered by drone…the guest of honor's personal cake. The crowd was properly impressed as it flew down from the heavens in a bright ball of fiery candles, which Ricky blew out with a wink at Dana and a coy joke that he hoped his wish would come true that night.

Dessert was just winding down as Ricky stood and clinked his fork against his champagne glass to get everyone's attention.

He cleared his throat before continuing. "First off, I want to thank you for being here. I'm deeply humbled and honored that you're all here to celebrate my birthday."

This earned him a round of applause from the crowd.

"And," he went on, "I want to thank Dana for all the hard work—"

"And secrecy!" she interjected, laughing.

"—and secrecy," Ricky agreed, "she had to keep up in order to pull this off. Thank you, honey." He pulled her close and gave her a sweet kiss on the lips that had everyone erupting into applause again.

Once he pulled back, he addressed the room again. "However, I've actually been engaging in some secrecy myself."

Dana frowned at him.

"And I have a little something for you, Dana."

"M-me?" she said, clearly taken aback.

Ricky nodded, a mischievous gleam in his eyes.

"But it's *your* birthday," she protested. Her eyes cut to me in a questioning gaze.

I shrugged. Honestly, I had no idea what Ricky had up his sleeve. Thankfully, for once, I was out of the loop.

"I know, I know," Ricky said. "But, there's something I've been promising you for some time now. And I want to make good on that promise." He held up her left hand, letting her engagement ring catch the light.

"As many of you know," Ricky said to the crowd, "Dana and I have been engaged for quite some time. And some might even say I've been dragging my feet when it comes to setting a wedding date."

"I'll say!" someone in the crowd shouted. Which caused a ripple of laughter again.

Ricky grinned in response and nodded. "But no more dragging," he told us.

Dana blinked at him. "You're setting a wedding date?" she asked. I could hear the lift of hope in her voice.

Ricky's grin grew wider as he turned to face her and nodded slowly. "Yes. Which is why I wanted all of your friends and family to be here."

Dana did a squeal and clapped. The crowd clapped along with her.

"Okay, lay it on me. When do we tie the knot?" she asked Ricky.

I swore if his grin grew any wider, he'd need another set of teeth as he answered, "Right now."

Dana blinked at him. "N-now?"

"Now."

Out of nowhere, someone handed Dana a bridal bouquet. The quartet suddenly started playing the wedding march. Lights at the adjacent patio went on, illuminating a makeshift altar swathed in flowers that I swore had appeared out of thin air. Or maybe more accurately, out of Marco's devious little party planning book.

Speaking of which, Marco stood at the altar, a book opened in his hands, looking ready to officiate.

"Dana," Ricky said, suddenly bending to one knee. "Will you marry me *right now*?"

I had to admit, I was probably wearing a huge grin myself right about then. As Dana tearfully nodded yes, the crowd cheered.

Dana's dad appeared from the sidelines, taking her by the arm as he walked her through the crowd, who'd parted to create a makeshift aisle. I watched Dana and Ricky stare at each other like two lovestruck teenagers throughout the short but sweet ceremony, until Marco finally pronounced them husband and wife. They sealed the deal with a kiss, and I felt myself tearing up.

"Tell me you didn't know about this?" Ramirez said, clapping beside me to celebrate the newlywed couple.

I shook my head. "Scouts honor, I had no idea." But I did know one thing—Marco had pulled off the best surprise Dana could have hoped for.

"They're kinda cute together," Ramirez added.

I glanced up to see his eyes misting as he took in the happy couple. "Jackson Wyoming Ramirez, you're not crying, are you?"

He grinned at me. "God, no. What do you think I am, a softy?"

I couldn't help grinning right back. "Shut up and kiss me, you old softy."

"With pleasure, Ms. Springer."

And he did.

Oh boy, did he.

ABOUT THE AUTHOR

Gemma Halliday is the #1 Amazon, *New York Times* & *USA Today* bestselling author of several mystery series. Gemma's books have received numerous awards, including a Golden Heart, two National Reader's Choice awards, three RITA nominations, a RONE award for best mystery, and two Killer Nashville Silver Falchion Awards for best cozy mystery and readers' choice. She currently lives in the San Francisco Bay Area with her large, loud, and loving family.

To learn more about Gemma, visit her online at www.GemmaHalliday.com

The High Heels Mysteries

www.GemmaHalliday.com

Made in the USA
Las Vegas, NV
05 September 2024